PENGUIN BOOKS

THE MOON IS DOWN

John Steinbeck was born in Salinas, California, in 1902. The town is a few miles from the Pacific Coast and near the fertile Salinas Valley—an area that was to be the background of much of his fiction. He studied marine biology at Stanford University but left without taking a degree and, after a series of laboring jobs, began to write. An attempt at a free-lance literary career in New York failed, and he returned to California, continuing to write in a lonely cottage. Popular success came to him only in 1935 with *Tortilla Flat*. That book's promise was confirmed by succeeding works—*In Dubious Battle, Of Mice and Men,* and especially *The Grapes of Wrath,* a novel so powerful that it remains among the archetypes of American culture. Often set in California, Steinbeck's later books included *Cannery Row, The Wayward Bus, East of Eden, The Short Reign of Pippin IV,* and *Travels with Charley.* He died in 1968, having won a Nobel Prize in 1962. In announcing the award, the Swedish Academy declared: "He had no mind to be an unoffending comforter and entertainer. Instead, the topics he chose were serious and denunciatory, for instance the bitter strikes on California's fruit and cotton plantations. . . . His literary power steadily gained impetus. . . . The little masterpiece *Of Mice and Men* . . . was followed by those incomparable short stories which he collected together in the volume *The Long Valley.* The way had now been paved for the great work . . . the epic chronicle *The Grapes of Wrath.*"

BY JOHN STEINBECK

FICTION

Cup of Gold
The Pastures of Heaven
To a God Unknown
Tortilla Flat
In Dubious Battle
Saint Katy the Virgin
Of Mice and Men
The Red Pony
The Long Valley
The Grapes of Wrath
The Moon Is Down

Cannery Row
The Wayward Bus
The Pearl
Burning Bright
(*play in story form*)
East of Eden
Sweet Thursday
The Winter of Our Discontent
The Short Reign of Pippin IV:
A Fabrication

NONFICTION

Sea of Cortez: A Leisurely Journal of Travel and Research
(*in collaboration with Edward F. Ricketts*)
Bombs Away: The Story of a Bomber Team
A Russian Journal (*with pictures by Robert Capa*)
The Log from the *Sea of Cortez*
Once There Was a War
Travels with Charley in Search of America
America and Americans
Journal of a Novel: The *East of Eden* Letters

PLAYS,
A DOCUMENTARY,
AND
A SCREENPLAY

Of Mice and Men
The Moon Is Down
The Forgotten Village
Viva Zapata!

COLLECTIONS
The Portable Steinbeck
The Short Novels of
John Steinbeck
Steinbeck: A Life in Letters

CRITICAL LIBRARY EDITION
The Grapes of Wrath
(*edited by Peter Lisca*)

THE MOON
IS DOWN

A NOVEL

By John Steinbeck

PENGUIN BOOKS

Penguin Books Ltd, Harmondsworth,
Middlesex, England
Penguin Books, 625 Madison Avenue,
New York, New York 10022, U.S.A.
Penguin Books Australia Ltd, Ringwood,
Victoria, Australia
Penguin Books Canada Limited, 2801 John Street,
Markham, Ontario, Canada L3R 1B4
Penguin Books (N.Z.) Ltd, 182–190 Wairau Road,
Auckland 10, New Zealand

First published in the United States of America by
The Viking Press 1942
Viking Compass Edition published 1970
Reprinted 1974
Published in Penguin Books 1982
Reprinted 1982

LIBRARY OF CONGRESS CATALOGING IN PUBLICATION DATA
Steinbeck, John, 1902–1968.
The moon is down.
Reprint. Originally published: New York:
Viking Press, 1942.
I. Title.
[PS3537.T3234M6 1982] 813'.52 81-23470
ISBN 0 14 00.6222 X   AACR2

Printed in the United States of America by
Offset Paperback Mfrs., Inc., Dallas, Pennsylvania
Set in Caledonia

THE MOON IS DOWN

CHAPTER ONE

By TEN-FORTY-FIVE it was all over. The town was occupied, the defenders defeated, and the war finished. The invader had prepared for this campaign as carefully as he had for larger ones. On this Sunday morning the postman and the policeman had gone fishing in the boat of Mr. Corell, the popular storekeeper. He had lent them his trim sailboat for the day. The postman and the policeman were several miles at sea when they saw the small, dark transport, loaded with soldiers, go quietly past them. As officials of the town, this was definitely their business, and these two put about, but of course the battalion was in possession by the time they could make port. The policeman and the postman could not even get into their own offices in the Town Hall, and when they insisted on their rights they were taken prisoners of war and locked up in the town jail.

The local troops, all twelve of them, had been away, too, on this Sunday morning, for Mr. Corell, the popular storekeeper, had donated lunch, targets, cartridges, and prizes for a shooting-competition to take place six miles back in the hills, in a lovely glade Mr. Corell owned. The local troops, big, loose-hung boys, heard the planes and in the distance saw the parachutes, and they came back to town at double-quick step. When they arrived, the invader had flanked the road with machine guns. The loose-hung soldiers, having very little experience in war and none at all in defeat, opened fire with their rifles. The machine guns clattered for a moment and six of the soldiers became dead riddled bundles and three, half-dead riddled bundles, and three of the soldiers escaped into the hills with their rifles.

By ten-thirty the brass band of the invader was playing beautiful and sentimental music in the town square while the townsmen, their mouths a little open and their eyes astonished, stood about listening to the music and staring at the gray-helmeted men who carried sub-machine guns in their arms.

By ten-thirty-eight the riddled six were buried, the parachutes were folded, and the battalion was billeted in Mr. Corell's warehouse by the pier, which had on its shelves blankets and cots for a battalion.

By ten-forty-five old Mayor Orden had received the formal request that he grant an audience to Colonel Lanser of the invaders, an audience which was set for eleven sharp at the Mayor's five-room palace.

The drawing-room of the palace was very sweet and comfortable. The gilded chairs covered with their worn tapestry were set about stiffly like too many servants with nothing to do. An arched marble fireplace held its little basket of red flameless heat, and a hand-painted coal scuttle stood on the hearth. On the mantel, flanked by fat vases, stood a large, curly porcelain clock which swarmed with tumbling cherubs. The wallpaper of the room was dark red with gold figures, and the woodwork was white, pretty, and clean. The paintings on the wall were largely preoccupied with the amazing heroism of large dogs faced with imperiled children. Nor water nor fire nor earthquake could do in a child so long as a big dog was available.

Beside the fireplace old Doctor Winter sat, bearded and simple and benign, historian and physician to the town. He watched in amazement while his thumbs rolled over and over on his lap. Doctor Winter was a man so simple that only a profound man would know him as profound. He looked up at Joseph, the Mayor's servingman, to see whether Joseph had observed the rolling wonders of his thumbs.

"Eleven o'clock?" Doctor Winter asked.

And Joseph answered abstractedly, "Yes, sir. The note said eleven."

"You read the note?"

"No, sir, His Excellency read the note to me."

And Joseph went about testing each of the gilded chairs to see whether it had moved since he had last placed it. Joseph habitually scowled at furniture, expecting it to be impertinent, mischievous, or dusty. In a world where Mayor Orden was the leader of men, Joseph was the leader of furniture, silver, and dishes. Joseph was elderly and lean and serious, and his life was so complicated that only a profound man would know him to be simple. He saw nothing amazing about Doctor Winter's rolling thumbs; in fact he found them irritating. Joseph suspected that something pretty important was happening, what with foreign soldiers in the town and the local army killed or captured. Sooner or later Joseph would have to get an opinion about it all. He wanted no levity, no rolling thumbs, no nonsense from furniture. Doctor Winter moved his chair a few inches from its appointed place and Joseph waited impatiently for the moment when he could put it back again.

Doctor Winter repeated, "Eleven o'clock, and they'll be here then, too. A time-minded people, Joseph."

And Joseph said, without listening, "Yes, sir."

"A time-minded people," the doctor repeated.

"Yes, sir," said Joseph.

"Time and machines."

"Yes, sir."

"They hurry toward their destiny as though it would not wait. They push the rolling world along with their shoulders."

And Joseph said, "Quite right, sir," simply because he was getting tired of saying, "Yes, sir."

Joseph did not approve of this line of conversation, since it did not help him to have an opinion about anything. If Joseph remarked to the cook later in the day, "A time-minded people, Annie," it would not make any sense. Annie would ask, "Who?" and then "Why?" and finally say, "That's nonsense, Joseph." Joseph had tried carrying Doctor Winter's remarks below-stairs before and it had always ended the same: Annie always discovered them to be nonsense.

Doctor Winter looked up from his thumbs and watched Joseph disciplining the chairs. "What's the Mayor doing?"

"Dressing to receive the colonel, sir."

"And you aren't helping him? He will be ill dressed by himself."

"Madame is helping him. Madame wants him to look his best. She"—Joseph blushed a little—"Madame is trimming the hair out of his ears, sir. It tickles. He won't let me do it."

"Of course it tickles," said Doctor Winter.

"Madame insists," said Joseph.

Doctor Winter laughed suddenly. He stood up and

held his hands to the fire and Joseph skillfully darted behind him and replaced the chair where it should be.

"We are so wonderful," the doctor said. "Our country is falling, our town is conquered, the Mayor is about to receive the conqueror, and Madame is holding the struggling Mayor by the neck and trimming the hair out of his ears."

"He was getting very shaggy," said Joseph. "His eyebrows, too. His Excellency is even more upset about having his eyebrows trimmed than his ears. He says it hurts. I doubt if even Madame can do it."

"She will try," Doctor Winter said.

"She wants him to look his best, sir."

Through the glass window of the entrance door a helmeted face looked in and there was a rapping on the door. It seemed that some warm light went out of the room and a little grayness took its place.

Doctor Winter looked up at the clock and said, "They are early. Let them in, Joseph."

Joseph went to the door and opened it. A soldier stepped in, dressed in a long coat. He was helmeted and he carried a sub-machine gun over his arm. He glanced quickly about and then stepped aside. Behind him an officer stood in the doorway. The officer's uniform was common and it had rank showing only on the shoulders.

The officer stepped inside and looked at Doctor Winter. He was rather like an overdrawn picture of an English gentleman. He had a slouch, his face was red, his nose long but rather pleasing; he seemed about as unhappy in his uniform as most British general officers are. He stood in the doorway, staring at Doctor Winter, and he said, "Are you Mayor Orden, sir?"

Doctor Winter smiled. "No, no, I am not."

"You are an official, then?"

"No, I am the town doctor and I am a friend of the Mayor."

The officer said, "Where is Mayor Orden?"

"Dressing to receive you. You are the colonel?"

"No, I am not. I am Captain Bentick." He bowed and Doctor Winter returned the bow slightly. Captain Bentick continued, as though a little embarrassed at what he had to say. "Our military regulations, sir, prescribe that we search for weapons before the commanding officer enters a room. We mean no disrespect, sir." And he called over his shoulder, "Sergeant!"

The sergeant moved quickly to Joseph, ran his hands over his pockets, and said, "Nothing, sir."

Captain Bentick said to Doctor Winter, "I hope you will pardon us." And the sergeant went to Doctor Winter and patted his pockets. His hands stopped at the inside coat pocket. He reached quickly in, brought out a little, flat, black leather case, and took it to Captain Bentick. Captain Bentick opened the case and found there a few simple surgical instruments—two scalpels, some surgical needles, some clamps, a hypodermic needle. He closed the case again and handed it back to Doctor Winter.

Doctor Winter said, "You see, I am a country doctor. One time I had to perform an appendectomy with a kitchen knife. I have always carried these with me since then."

Captain Bentick said, "I believe there are some firearms here?" He opened a little leather book that he carried in his pocket.

Doctor Winter said, "You are thorough."

"Yes, our local man has been working here for some time."

Doctor Winter said, "I don't suppose you would tell who that man is?"

Bentick said, "His work is all done now. I don't suppose there would be any harm in telling. His name is Corell."

And Doctor Winter said in astonishment, "George Corell? Why, that seems impossible! He's done a lot for this town. Why, he even gave prizes for the shooting-match in the hills this morning." And as he said it his eyes began to understand what had happened and his mouth closed slowly, and he said, "I see; that is why he gave the shooting-match. Yes, I see. But George Corell—that sounds impossible!"

The door to the left opened and Mayor Orden came in; he was digging in his right ear with his little finger. He was dressed in his official morning coat, with his chain of office about his neck. He had a large, white, spraying mustache and two smaller ones, one over each eye. His white hair was so recently brushed that only now were the hairs struggling to be free, to stand up again. He had been Mayor so long that he was the Idea-Mayor in the town. Even grown people when they saw the word "mayor," printed or written, saw Mayor Orden in their minds. He and his office were one. It had given him dignity and he had given it warmth.

From behind him Madame emerged, small and wrinkled and fierce. She considered that she had created this man out of whole cloth, had thought him up, and she was sure that she could do a better job if she had it to do again. Only once or twice in her life had she ever understood all of him, but the part of him which she knew, she knew intricately and well. No little appetite or pain, no carelessness or meanness in him escaped her; no thought or dream or longing in him ever reached her. And yet several times in her life she had seen the stars.

She stepped around the Mayor and she took his hand and pulled his finger out of his outraged ear and pushed his hand to his side, the way she would take a baby's thumb away from his mouth.

[21]

"I don't believe for a moment it hurts as much as you say," she said, and to Doctor Winter, "He won't let me fix his eyebrows."

"It hurts," said Mayor Orden.

"Very well, if you want to look like that there is nothing I can do about it." She straightened his already straight tie. "I'm glad you're here, Doctor," she said. "How many do you think will come?" And then she looked up and saw Captain Bentick. "Oh," she said, "the colonel!"

Captain Bentick said, "No, ma'am, I'm only preparing for the colonel. Sergeant!"

The sergeant, who had been turning over pillows, looking behind pictures, came quickly to Mayor Orden and ran his hands over his pockets.

Captain Bentick said, "Excuse him, sir, it's regulations."

He glanced again at the little book in his hand. "Your Excellency, I think you have firearms here. Two items, I believe?"

Mayor Orden said, "Firearms? Guns, you mean, I guess. Yes, I have a shotgun and a sporting-rifle." He said deprecatingly, "You know, I don't hunt very much any more. I always think I'm going to, and then the season opens and I don't get out. I don't take the pleasure in it I used to."

Captain Bentick insisted. "Where are these guns, Your Excellency?"

The Mayor rubbed his cheek and tried to think. "Why, I think—" He turned to Madame. "Weren't they in the back of that cabinet in the bedroom with the walking-sticks?"

Madame said, "Yes, and every stitch of clothing in that cabinet smells of oil. I wish you'd put them somewhere else."

Captain Bentick said, "Sergeant!" and the sergeant went quickly into the bedroom.

"It's an unpleasant duty. I'm sorry," said the captain.

The sergeant came back, carrying a double-barreled shotgun and a rather nice sporting-rifle with a shoulder strap. He leaned them against the side of the entrance door.

Captain Bentick said, "That's all, thank you, Your Excellency. Thank you, Madame."

He turned and bowed slightly to Doctor Winter. "Thank you, Doctor. Colonel Lanser will be here directly. Good morning!"

And he went out of the front door, followed by the sergeant with the two guns in one hand and the sub-machine gun over his right arm.

Madame said, "For a moment I thought he was the colonel. He was a rather nice-looking young man."

Doctor Winter said sardonically, "No, he was just protecting the colonel."

Madame was thinking, "I wonder how many officers will come?" And she looked at Joseph and saw that he was shamelessly eavesdropping. She shook her head at him and frowned and he went back to the little things he had been doing. He began dusting all over again.

And Madame said, "How many do you think will come?"

Doctor Winter pulled out a chair outrageously and sat down again. "I don't know," he said.

"Well"—she frowned at Joseph—"we've been talking it over. Should we offer them tea or a glass of wine? If we do, I don't know how many there will be, and if we don't, what are we to do?"

Doctor Winter shook his head and smiled. "I don't know. It's been so long since we conquered anybody or anybody conquered us. I don't know what is proper."

Mayor Orden had his finger back in his itching ear. He said, "Well, I don't think we should. I don't think the people would like it. I don't want to drink wine with them. I don't know why."

Madame appealed to the doctor then. "Didn't people in the old days—the leaders, that is—compliment each other and take a glass of wine?"

Doctor Winter nodded. "Yes, indeed they did." He shook his head slowly. "Maybe that was different. Kings and princes played at war the way Englishmen play at hunting. When the fox was dead they gathered at a hunt breakfast. But Mayor Orden is probably right: the people might not like him to drink wine with the invader."

Madame said, "The people are down listening to the music. Annie told me. If they can do that, why shouldn't we keep civilized procedure alive?"

The Mayor looked steadily at her for a moment and his voice was sharp. "Madame, I think with your per-

mission we will not have wine. The people are confused now. They have lived at peace so long that they
do not quite believe in war. They will learn and then
they will not be confused any more. They elected me
not to be confused. Six town boys were murdered this
morning. I think we will have no hunt breakfast. The
people do not fight wars for sport."

Madame bowed slightly. There had been a number
of times in her life when her husband had become the
Mayor. She had learned not to confuse the Mayor with
her husband.

Mayor Orden looked at his watch and when Joseph
came in, carrying a small cup of black coffee, he took
it absent-mindedly. "Thank you," he said, and he
sipped it. "I should be clear," he said apologetically
to Doctor Winter. "I should be—do you know how
many men the invader has?"

"Not many," the doctor said. "I don't think over two
hundred and fifty; but all with those little machine
guns."

The Mayor sipped his coffee again and made a new
start. "What about the rest of the country?"

The doctor raised his shoulders and dropped them again.

"Was there no resistance anywhere?" the Mayor went on hopelessly.

And again the doctor raised his shoulders. "I don't know. The wires are cut or captured. There is no news."

"And our boys, our soldiers?"

"I don't know," said the doctor.

Joseph interrupted. "I heard—that is, Annie heard—"

"What, Joseph?"

"Six men were killed, sir, by the machine guns. Annie heard three were wounded and captured."

"But there were twelve."

"Annie heard that three escaped."

The Mayor turned sharply. "Which ones escaped?" he demanded.

"I don't know, sir. Annie didn't hear."

Madame inspected a table for dust with her finger. She said, "Joseph, when they come, stay close to your bell. We might want some little thing. And put on

your other coat, Joseph, the one with the buttons."
She thought for a moment. "And, Joseph, when you
finish what you are told to do, go out of the room.
It makes a bad impression when you just stand around
listening. It's provincial, that's what it is."

"Yes, Madame," Joseph said.

"We won't serve wine, Joseph, but you might have
some cigarettes handy in that little silver conserve box.
And don't strike the match to light the colonel's cigarette on your shoe. Strike it on the match-box."

"Yes, Madame."

Mayor Orden unbuttoned his coat and took out his
watch and looked at it and put it back and buttoned
his coat again, one button too high. Madame went to
him and rebuttoned it correctly.

Doctor Winter asked, "What time is it?"

"Five of eleven."

"A time-minded people," the doctor said. "They will
be here on time. Do you want me to go away?"

Mayor Orden looked startled. "Go? No—no, stay."
He laughed softly. "I'm a little afraid," he said apologetically. "Well, not afraid, but I'm nervous." And he
said helplessly, "We have never been conquered, for

a long time—" He stopped to listen. In the distance there was a sound of band music, a march. They all turned in its direction and listened.

Madame said, "Here they come. I hope not too many try to crowd in here at once. It isn't a very big room."

Doctor Winter said sardonically, "Madame would prefer the Hall of Mirrors at Versailles?"

She pinched her lips and looked about, already placing the conquerors with her mind. "It is a very small room," she said.

The band music swelled a little and then grew fainter. There came a gentle tap on the door.

"Now, who can that be? Joseph, if it is anyone, tell him to come back later. We are very busy."

The tap came again. Joseph went to the door and opened it a crack and then a little wider. A gray figure, helmeted and gantleted, appeared.

"Colonel Lanser's compliments," the head said. "Colonel Lanser requests an audience with Your Excellency."

Joseph opened the door wide. The helmeted orderly stepped inside and looked quickly about the room and then stood aside. "Colonel Lanser!" he announced.

A second helmeted figure walked into the room, and his rank showed only on his shoulders. Behind him came a rather short man in a black business suit. The colonel was a middle-aged man, gray and hard and tired-looking. He had the square shoulders of a soldier, but his eyes lacked the blank look of the ordinary soldier. The little man beside him was bald and rosy-cheeked, with small black eyes and a sensual mouth.

Colonel Lanser took off his helmet. With a quick bow, he said, "Your Excellency!" He bowed to Madame. "Madame!" And he said, "Close the door, please, Corporal." Joseph quickly shut the door and stared in small triumph at the soldier.

Lanser looked questioningly at the doctor, and Mayor Orden said, "This is Doctor Winter."

"An official?" the colonel asked.

"A doctor, sir, and, I might say, the local historian."

Lanser bowed slightly. He said, "Doctor Winter, I do not mean to be impertinent, but there will be a page in your history, perhaps——"

And Doctor Winter smiled. "Many pages, perhaps."

Colonel Lanser turned slightly toward his companion. "I think you know Mr. Corell," he said.

The Mayor said, "George Corell? Of course I know him. How are you, George?"

Doctor Winter cut in sharply. He said, very formally, "Your Excellency, our friend, George Corell, prepared this town for the invasion. Our benefactor, George Corell, sent our soldiers into the hills. Our dinner guest, George Corell, has made a list of every firearm in the town. Our friend, George Corell!"

Corell said angrily, "I work for what I believe in! That is an honorable thing."

Orden's mouth hung a little open. He was bewildered. He looked helplessly from Winter to Corell. "This isn't true," he said. "George, this isn't true! You have sat at my table, you have drunk port with me. Why, you helped me plan the hospital! This isn't true!"

He was looking very steadily at Corell and Corell looked belligerently back at him. There was a long silence. Then the Mayor's face grew slowly tight and very formal and his whole body was rigid. He turned to Colonel Lanser and he said, "I do not wish to speak in this gentleman's company."

Corell said, "I have a right to be here! I am a soldier like the rest. I simply do not wear a uniform."

The Mayor repeated, "I do not wish to speak in this gentleman's presence."

Colonel Lanser said, "Will you leave us now, Mr. Corell?"

And Corell said, "I have a right to be here!"

Lanser repeated sharply, "Will you leave us now, Mr. Corell? Do you outrank me?"

"Well, no, sir."

"Please go, Mr. Corell," said Colonel Lanser.

And Corell looked at the Mayor angrily, and then he turned and went quickly out of the doorway. Doctor Winter chuckled and said, "That's good enough for a paragraph in my history." Colonel Lanser glanced sharply at him but he did not speak.

Now the door on the right opened, and straw-haired, red-eyed Annie put an angry face into the doorway. "There's soldiers on the back porch, Madame," she said. "Just standing there."

"They won't come in," Colonel Lanser said. "It's only military procedure."

Madame said icily, "Annie, if you have anything to say, let Joseph bring the message."

"I didn't know but they'd try to get in," Annie said. "They smelled the coffee."

"Annie!"

"Yes, Madame," and she withdrew.

The colonel said, "May I sit down?" And he explained, "We have been a long time without sleep."

The Mayor seemed to start out of sleep himself. "Yes," he said, "of course, sit down!"

The colonel looked at Madame and she seated herself and he settled tiredly into a chair. Mayor Orden stood, still half dreaming.

The colonel began, "We want to get along as well as we can. You see, sir, this is more like a business venture than anything else. We need the coal mine here and the fishing. We will try to get along with just as little friction as possible."

The Mayor said, "I have had no news. What about the rest of the country?"

"All taken," said the colonel. "It was well planned."

"Was there no resistance anywhere?"

The colonel looked at him compassionately. "I wish there had not been. Yes, there was some resistance, but it only caused bloodshed. We had planned very carefully."

Orden stuck to his point. "But there was resistance?"

"Yes, but it was foolish to resist. Just as here, it was destroyed instantly. It was sad and foolish to resist."

Doctor Winter caught some of the Mayor's anxiousness about the point. "Yes," he said, "foolish, but they resisted?"

And Colonel Lanser replied, "Only a few and they are gone. The people as a whole are quiet."

Doctor Winter said, "The people don't know yet what has happened."

"They are discovering," said Lanser. "They won't be foolish again." He cleared his throat and his voice became brisk. "Now, sir, I must get to business. I'm really very tired, but before I can sleep I must make my arrangements." He sat forward in his chair. "I am more engineer than soldier. This whole thing is more an engineering job than conquest. The coal must come out of the ground and be shipped. We have technicians, but the local people will continue to work the mine. Is that clear? We do not wish to be harsh."

And Orden said, "Yes, that's clear enough. But suppose the people do not want to work the mine?"

The colonel said, "I hope they will want to, because
they must. We must have the coal."

"But if they don't?"

"They must. They are an orderly people. They don't
want trouble." He waited for the Mayor's reply and
none came. "Is that not so, sir?" the colonel asked.

Mayor Orden twisted his chain. "I don't know, sir.
They are orderly under their own government. I don't
know how they would be under yours. It is untouched
ground, you see. We have built our government over
four hundred years."

The colonel said quickly, "We know that, and so
we are going to keep your government. You will still
be the Mayor, you will give the orders, you will penal-
ize and reward. In that way, they will not give trouble."

Mayor Orden looked at Doctor Winter. "What are
you thinking about?"

"I don't know," said Doctor Winter. "It would be in-
teresting to see. I'd expect trouble. This might be a
bitter people."

Mayor Orden said, "I don't know, either." He turned to the colonel. "Sir, I am of this people, and yet I don't know what they will do. Perhaps you know. Or maybe it would be different from anything you know or we know. Some people accept appointed leaders and obey them. But my people have elected me. They made me and they can unmake me. Perhaps they will if they think I have gone over to you. I just don't know."

The colonel said, "You will be doing them a service if you keep them in order."

"A service?"

"Yes, a service. It is your duty to protect them from harm. They will be in danger if they are rebellious. We must get the coal, you see. Our leaders do not tell us how; they order us to get it. But you have your people to protect. You must make them do the work and thus keep them safe."

Mayor Orden asked, "But suppose they don't want to be safe?"

"Then you must think for them."

Orden said, a little proudly, "My people don't like to have others think for them. Maybe they are different from your people. I am confused, but that I am sure of."

Now Joseph came in quickly and he stood leaning forward, bursting to speak. Madame said, "What is it, Joseph? Get the silver box of cigarettes."

"Pardon, Madame," said Joseph. "Pardon, Your Excellency."

"What do you want?" the Mayor asked.

"It's Annie," he said. "She's getting angry, sir."

"What is the matter?" Madame demanded.

"Annie doesn't like the soldiers on the back porch."

The colonel asked, "Are they causing trouble?"

"They are looking through the door at Annie," said Joseph. "She hates that."

The colonel said, "They are carrying out orders. They are doing no harm."

"Well, Annie hates to be stared at," said Joseph.

Madame said, "Joseph, tell Annie to take care."

"Yes, Madame," and Joseph went out.

The colonel's eyes dropped with tiredness. "There's another thing, Your Excellency," he said. "Would it be possible for me and my staff to stay here?"

Mayor Orden thought a moment and he said, "It's a small place. There are larger, more comfortable places."

Then Joseph came back with the silver box of cigarettes and he opened it and held it in front of the colonel. When the colonel took one, Joseph ostentatiously lighted it. The colonel puffed deeply.

"It isn't that," he said. "We have found that when a staff lives under the roof of the local authority, there is more tranquillity."

"You mean," said Orden, "the people feel there is collaboration involved?"

"Yes, I suppose that is it."

Mayor Orden looked hopelessly at Doctor Winter, and Winter could offer him nothing but a wry smile. Orden said softly, "Am I permitted to refuse this honor?"

"I'm sorry," the colonel said. "No. These are the orders of my leader."

"The people will not like it," Orden said.

"Always the people! The people are disarmed. The people have no say."

Mayor Orden shook his head. "You do not know, sir."

From the doorway came the sound of an angry woman's voice, and a thump and a man's cry. Joseph came scuttling through the door. "She's thrown boiling water," Joseph said. "She's very angry."

There were commands through the door and the clump of feet. Colonel Lanser got up heavily. "Have you no control over your servants, sir?" he asked.

Mayor Orden smiled. "Very little," he said. "She's a good cook when she is happy. Was anyone hurt?" he asked Joseph.

"The water was boiling, sir."

Colonel Lanser said, "We just want to do our job. It's an engineering job. You will have to discipline your cook."

"I can't," said Orden. "She'll quit."

"This is an emergency. She can't quit."

"Then she'll throw water," said Doctor Winter.

The door opened and a soldier stood in the opening. "Shall I arrest this woman, sir?"

"Was anyone hurt?" Lanser asked.

"Yes, sir, scalded, and one man bitten. We are holding her, sir."

Lanser looked helpless, then he said, "Release her and go outside and off the porch."

"Yes, sir," and the door closed behind the soldier.

Lanser said, "I could have her shot; I could lock her up."

"Then we would have no cook," said Orden.

"Look," said the colonel. "We are instructed to get along with your people."

Madame said, "Excuse me, sir, I will just go and see if the soldiers hurt Annie," and she went out.

Now Lanser stood up. "I told you I'm very tired, sir. I must have some sleep. Please co-operate with us for the good of all." When Mayor Orden made no reply, "For the good of all," Lanser repeated. "Will you?"

Orden said, "This is a little town. I don't know. The people are confused and so am I."

"But will you try to co-operate?"

Orden shook his head. "I don't know. When the town makes up its mind what it wants to do, I'll probably do that."

"But you are the authority."

Orden smiled. "You won't believe this, but it is true: authority is in the town. I don't know how or why, but it is so. This means we cannot act as quickly as you can, but when a direction is set, we all act together. I am confused. I don't know yet."

Lanser said wearily, "I hope we can get along together. It will be so much easier for everyone. I hope we can trust you. I don't like to think of the means the military will take to keep order."

Mayor Orden was silent.

"I hope we can trust you," Lanser repeated.

Orden put his finger in his ear and wiggled his hand. "I don't know," he said.

Madame came through the door then. "Annie is furious," she said. "She is next door, talking to Christine. Christine is angry, too."

"Christine is even a better cook than Annie," said the Mayor.

CHAPTER TWO

Upstairs in the little palace of the Mayor the staff of Colonel Lanser made its headquarters. There were five of them besides the colonel. There was Major Hunter, a haunted little man of figures, a little man who, being a dependable unit, considered all other men either as dependable units or as unfit to live. Major Hunter was an engineer, and except in case of war no one would have thought of giving him command of men. For Major Hunter set his men in rows like figures and he added and subtracted and multiplied them. He was an arithmetician rather than a mathematician. None of the humor, the music, or the mysticism of higher mathematics ever entered his head. Men might vary in height or weight or color, just as 6 is different from 8, but there was little other difference. He had been married several times and he did not know why his wives became very nervous before they left him.

Captain Bentick was a family man, a lover of dogs and pink children and Christmas. He was too old to be a captain, but a curious lack of ambition had kept him in that rank. Before the war he had admired the British country gentleman very much, wore English clothes, kept English dogs, smoked in an English pipe a special pipe mixture sent him from London, and subscribed to those country magazines which extol gardening and continually argue about the relative merits of English and Gordon setters. Captain Bentick spent all his holidays in Sussex and liked to be mistaken for an Englishman in Budapest or Paris. The war changed all that outwardly, but he had sucked on a pipe too long, had carried a stick too long, to give them up too suddenly. Once, five years before, he had written a letter to the *Times* about grass dying in the Midlands and had signed it Edmund Twitchell, Esq.; and, furthermore, the *Times* had printed it.

If Captain Bentick was too old to be a captain, Captain Loft was too young. Captain Loft was as much a captain as one can imagine. He lived and breathed his captaincy. He had no unmilitary moments. A driving ambition forced him up through the grades. He rose like cream to the top of milk. He clicked his heels as perfectly as a dancer does. He knew every kind of military courtesy and insisted on using it all. Generals were afraid of him because he knew more about the deportment of a soldier than they did. Captain Loft thought and believed that a soldier is the highest development of animal life. If he considered God at all, he thought of Him as an old and honored general, retired and gray, living among remembered battles and putting wreaths on the graves of his lieutenants several times a year. Captain Loft believed that all women fall in love with a uniform and he did not see how it could be otherwise. In the normal course of events he would be a brigadier-general at forty-five and have his picture in the illustrated papers, flanked by tall, pale, masculine women wearing lacy picture hats.

Lieutenants Prackle and Tonder were snot-noses, undergraduates, lieutenants, trained in the politics of the day, believing the great new system invented by a

genius so great that they never bothered to verify its
results. They were sentimental young men, given to
tears and to furies. Lieutenant Prackle carried a lock
of hair in the back of his watch, wrapped in a bit of
blue satin, and the hair was constantly getting loose
and clogging the balance wheel, so that he wore a
wrist watch for telling time. Prackle was a dancing-
partner, a gay young man who nevertheless could
scowl like the Leader, could brood like the Leader.
He hated degenerate art and had destroyed several
canvases with his own hands. In cabarets he sometimes
made pencil sketches of his companions which were so
good that he had often been told he should have been
an artist. Prackle had several blond sisters of whom he
was so proud that he had on occasion caused a commo-
tion when he thought they had been insulted. The sisters were a little disturbed about it because they were
afraid someone might set out to prove the insults, which
would not have been hard to do. Lieutenant Prackle
spent nearly all his time off duty day-dreaming of
seducing Lieutenant Tonder's blond sister, a buxom
girl who loved to be seduced by older men who did not
muss her hair as Lieutenant Prackle did.

Lieutenant Tonder was a poet, a bitter poet who dreamed of perfect, ideal love of elevated young men for poor girls. Tonder was a dark romantic with a vision as wide as his experience. He sometimes spoke blank verse under his breath to imaginary dark women. He longed for death on the battlefield, with weeping parents in the background, and the Leader, brave but sad in the presence of the dying youth. He imagined his death very often, lighted by a fair setting sun which glinted on broken military equipment, his men standing silently around him, with heads sunk low, as over a fat cloud galloped the Valkyries, big-breasted, mothers and mistresses in one, while Wagnerian thunder crashed in the background. And he even had his dying words ready.

These were the men of the staff, each one playing war as children play "Run, Sheep, Run." Major Hunter thought of war as an arithmetical job to be done so he could get back to his fireplace; Captain Loft as the proper career of a properly brought-up young man; and Lieutenants Prackle and Tonder as a dreamlike thing in which nothing was very real. And their war so far had been play—fine weapons and fine planning against unarmed, planless enemies. They had lost no fights and suffered little hurt. They were, under pressure, capable of cowardice or courage, as everyone is. Of them all, only Colonel Lanser knew what war really is in the long run.

Lanser had been in Belgium and France twenty years before and he tried not to think what he knew—that war is treachery and hatred, the muddling of incompetent generals, the torture and killing and sickness and tiredness, until at last it is over and nothing has changed except for new weariness and new hatreds. Lanser told himself he was a soldier, given orders to carry out. He was not expected to question or to think, but only to carry out orders; and he tried to put aside the sick memories of the other war and the certainty that this would be the same. This one will be different, he said to himself fifty times a day; this one will be very different.

In marching, in mobs, in football games, and in war, outlines become vague; real things become unreal and a fog creeps over the mind. Tension and excitement, weariness, movement—all merge in one great gray dream, so that when it is over, it is hard to remember how it was when you killed men or ordered them to be killed. Then other people who were not there tell you what it was like and you say vaguely, "Yes, I guess that's how it was."

This staff had taken three rooms on the upper floor of the Mayor's palace. In the bedrooms they had put their cots and blankets and equipment, and in the room next to them and directly over the little drawing-room on the ground floor they had made a kind of club, rather an uncomfortable club. There were a few chairs and a table. Here they wrote letters and read letters. They talked and ordered coffee and planned and rested. On the walls between the windows there were pictures of cows and lakes and little farmhouses, and from the windows they could look down over the town to the waterfront, to the docks where the shipping was tied up, to the docks where the coal barges pulled up and took their loads and went out to sea. They could look down over the little town that twisted past the square to the waterfront, and they could see the fishing-boats lying at anchor in the bay, the sails furled, and they could smell the drying fish on the beach, right through the window.

There was a large table in the center of the room and Major Hunter sat beside it. He had his drawing-board in his lap and resting on the table, and with a T-square and triangle he worked at a design for a new railroad siding. The drawing-board was unsteady and the major was growing angry with its unsteadiness. He called over his shoulder, "Prackle!" And then, "Lieutenant Prackle!"

The bedroom door opened and the lieutenant came out, half his face covered with shaving-cream. He held the brush in his hand. "Yes?" he said.

Major Hunter jiggled his drawing-board. "Hasn't that tripod for my board turned up in the baggage?"

"I don't know, sir," said Prackle. "I didn't look."

"Well, look now, will you? It's bad enough to have to work in this light. I'll have to draw this again before I ink it."

Prackle said, "Just as soon as I finish shaving, I'll look."

Hunter said irritably, "This siding is more important than your looks. See if there is a canvas case like a golf bag under that pile in there."

Prackle disappeared into the bedroom. The door to

the right opened and Captain Loft came in. He wore his helmet, a pair of field glasses, sidearm, and various little leather cases strung all over him. He began to remove his equipment as soon as he entered.

"You know, that Bentick's crazy," he said. "He was going out on duty in a fatigue cap, right down the street."

Loft put his field glasses on the table and took off his helmet, then his gas-mask bag. A little pile of equipment began to heap up on the table.

Hunter said, "Don't leave that stuff there. I have to work here. Why shouldn't he wear a cap? There hasn't been any trouble. I get sick of these tin things. They're heavy and you can't see."

Loft said primly, "It's bad practice to leave it off. It's bad for the people here. We must maintain a military standard, an alertness, and never vary it. We'll just invite trouble if we don't."

"What makes you think so?" Hunter asked.

Loft drew himself up a little. His mouth thinned with certainty. Sooner or later everyone wanted to punch Loft in the nose for his sureness about things. He said, "I don't think it. I was paraphrasing *Manual*

X-12 on deportment in occupied countries. It is very carefully worked out." He began to say, "You—" and then changed it to, "Everybody should read *X-12* very closely."

Hunter said, "I wonder whether the man who wrote it was ever in occupied country. These people are harmless enough. They seem to be good, obedient people."

Prackle came through the door, his face still half covered with shaving-soap. He carried a brown canvas tube, and behind him came Lieutenant Tonder. "Is this it?" Prackle asked.

"Yes. Unpack it, will you, and set it up."

Prackle and Tonder went to work on the folding tripod and tested it and put it near Hunter. The major screwed his board to it, tilted it right and left, and finally settled gruntingly behind it.

Captain Loft said, "Do you know you have soap on your face, Lieutenant?"

"Yes, sir," Prackle said. "I was shaving when the major asked me to get the tripod."

"Well, you had better get it off," Loft said. "The colonel might see you."

"Oh, he wouldn t mind. He doesn't care about things like that."

Tonder was looking over Hunter's shoulder as he worked.

Loft said, "Well, he may not, but it doesn't look right."

Prackle took a handkerchief and rubbed the soap from his cheek. Tonder pointed to a little drawing on the corner of the major's board. "That's a nice-looking bridge, Major. But where in the world are we going to build a bridge?"

Hunter looked down at the drawing and then over his shoulder at Tonder. "Huh? Oh, that isn't any bridge we're going to build. Up here is the work drawing."

"What are you doing with a bridge, then?"

Hunter seemed a little embarrassed. "Well, you know, in my back yard at home I've got a model railroad line. I was going to bridge a little creek for it. Brought the line right down to the creek, but I never did get the bridge built. I thought I'd kind of work it out while I was away."

Lieutenant Prackle took from his pocket a folded

rotogravure page and he unfolded it and held it up and looked at it. It was a picture of a girl, all legs and dress and eyelashes, a well-developed blonde in black openwork stockings and a low bodice, and this particular blonde peeped over a black lace fan. Lieutenant Prackle held her up and he said, "Isn't she something?" Lieutenant Tonder looked critically at the picture and said, "I don't like her."

"What don't you like about her?"

"I just don't like her," said Tonder. "What do you want her picture for?"

Prackle said, "Because I do like her and I bet you do, too."

"I do not," said Tonder.

"You mean to say you wouldn't take a date with her if you could?" Prackle asked.

Tonder said, "No."

"Well, you're just crazy," and Prackle went to one of the curtains. He said, "I'm just going to stick her up here and let you brood about her for a while." He pinned the picture to the curtain.

Captain Loft was gathering his equipment into his

arms now, and he said, "I don't think it looks very well out here, Lieutenant. You'd better take it down. It wouldn't make a good impression on the local people."

Hunter looked up from his board. "What wouldn't?" He followed their eyes to the picture. "Who's that?" he asked.

"She's an actress," said Prackle.

Hunter looked at her carefully. "Oh, do you know her?"

Tonder said, "She's a tramp."

Hunter said, "Oh, then you know her?"

Prackle was looking steadily at Tonder. He said, "Say, how do you know she's a tramp?"

"She looks like a tramp," said Tonder.

"Do you know her?"

"No, and I don't want to."

Prackle began to say, "Then how do you know?" when Loft broke in. He said, "You'd better take the picture down. Put it up over your bed if you want to. This room's kind of official here."

Prackle looked at him mutinously and was about to speak when Captain Loft said, "That's an order, Lieutenant," and poor Prackle folded his paper and put it into his pocket again. He tried cheerily to change the subject. "There are some pretty girls in this town, all right," he said. "As soon as we get settled down and everything going smoothly, I'm going to get acquainted with a few."

Loft said, "You'd better read *X-12*. There's a section dealing with sexual matters." And he went out, carrying his duffel, glasses, and equipment. Lieutenant Tonder, still looking over Hunter's shoulder, said, "That's clever—the coal cars come right through the mines to the ship."

Hunter came slowly out of his work and he said, "We have to speed it up; we've got to get that coal moving. It's a big job. I'm awful thankful that the people here are calm and sensible."

Loft came back into the room without his equipment. He stood by the window, looking out toward the harbor, toward the coal mine, and he said, "They are calm and sensible because we are calm and sensible. I think we can take credit for that. That's why I keep harping on procedure. It is very carefully worked out."

The door opened and Colonel Lanser came in, removing his coat as he entered. His staff gave him military courtesy—not very rigid, but enough. Lanser said, "Captain Loft, will you go down and relieve Bentick? He isn't feeling well, says he's dizzy."

"Yes, sir," said Loft. "May I suggest, sir, that I only recently came off duty?"

Lanser inspected him closely. "I hope you don't mind going, Captain."

"Not at all, sir; I just mention it for the record."

Lanser relaxed and chuckled. "You like to be mentioned in the reports, don't you?"

"It does no harm, sir."

"And when you have enough mentions," Lanser went on, "there will be a little dangler on your chest."

"They are the milestones in a military career, sir."

Lanser sighed. "Yes, I guess they are. But they won't be the ones you'll remember, Captain."

"Sir?" Loft asked.

"You'll know what I mean later—perhaps."

Captain Loft put his equipment on rapidly. "Yes, sir," he said, and went out and his footsteps clattered down the wooden stairs, and Lanser watched him go with a little amusement. He said quietly, "There goes a born soldier." And Hunter looked up and poised his pencil and he said, "A born ass."

"No," said Lanser, "he's being a soldier the way a lot of men would be politicians. He'll be on the General Staff before long. He'll look down on war from above and so he'll always love it."

Lieutenant Prackle said, "When do you think the war will be over, sir?"

"Over? Over? What do you mean?"

Lieutenant Prackle continued, "How soon will we win?"

Lanser shook his head. "Oh, I don't know. The enemy is still in the world."

"But we will lick them," said Prackle.

Lanser said, "Yes?"

"Won't we?"

"Yes; yes, we always do."

Prackle said excitedly, "Well, if it's quiet around Christmas, do you think there will be some furloughs granted?"

"I don't know," said Lanser. "Such orders will have to come from home. Do you want to get home for Christmas?"

"Well, I'd kind of like to."

"Maybe you will," said Lanser, "maybe you will."

Lieutenant Tonder said, "We won't drop out of this occupation, will we, sir, after the war is over?"

"I don't know," said the colonel. "Why?"

"Well," said Tonder, "it's a nice country, nice people. Our men—some of them—might even settle here."

Lanser said jokingly, "You've seen some place you like, perhaps?"

"Well," said Tonder, "there are some beautiful farms here. If four or five of them were thrown together, it would be a nice place to settle, I think."

"You have no family land, then?" Lanser asked.

"No, sir, not any more. Inflation took it away."

Lanser was tired now of talking to children. He said, "Ah, well, we still have a war to fight. We still have coal to take out. Do you suppose we can wait until it is over before we build up these estates? Such orders will come from above. Captain Loft can tell you that." His manner changed. He said, "Hunter, your steel will be in tomorrow. You can get your tracks started this week."

There was a knock at the door and a sentry put his head in. He said, "Mr. Corell wishes to see you, sir."

"Send him in," said the colonel. And he said to the others, "This is the man who did the preliminary work here. We might have some trouble with him."

"Did he do a good job?" Tonder asked.

"Yes, he did, and he won't be popular with the people here. I wonder whether he will be popular with us."

"He deserves credit, certainly," Tonder said.

"Yes," Lanser said, "and don't think he won't claim it."

Corell came in, rubbing his hands. He radiated good-will and good-fellowship. He was dressed still in his black business suit, but on his head there was a patch of white bandage, stuck to his hair with a cross of adhesive tape. He advanced to the center of the room and said, "Good morning, Colonel. I should have called yesterday after the trouble downstairs, but I knew how busy you would be."

The colonel said, "Good morning." Then with a circular gesture of his hand. "This is my staff, Mr. Corell."

"Fine boys," said Corell. "They did a good job. Well, I tried to prepare for them well."

Hunter looked down at his board and he took out an inking-pen and dipped it and began to ink in his drawing.

Lanser said, "You did very well. I wish you hadn't killed those six men, though. I wish their soldiers hadn't come back."

Corell spread his hands and said comfortably, "Six men is a small loss for a town of this size, with a coal mine, too."

Lanser said sternly, "I am not averse to killing people if that finishes it. But sometimes it is better not to."

Corell had been studying the officers. He looked sideways at the lieutenants, and he said, "Could we—perhaps—talk alone, Colonel?"

"Yes, if you wish. Lieutenant Prackle and Lieutenant Tonder, will you go to your room, please?" And the colonel said to Corell, "Major Hunter is working. He doesn't hear anything when he's working." Hunter looked up from his board and smiled quietly and looked down again. The young lieutenants left the room, and when they were gone Lanser said, "Well, here we are. Won't you sit down?"

"Thank you, sir," and Corell sat down behind the table.

Lanser looked at the bandage on Corell's head. He said bluntly, "Have they tried to kill you already?"

Corell felt the bandage with his fingers. "This? Oh, this was a stone that fell from a cliff in the hills this morning."

"You're sure it wasn't thrown?"

"What do you mean?" Corell asked. "These aren't fierce people. They haven't had a war for a hundred years. They've forgotten about fighting."

"Well, you've lived among them," said the colonel. "You ought to know." He stepped close to Corell. "But if you are safe, these people are different from any in the world. I've helped to occupy countries before. I was in Belgium twenty years ago and in France." He shook his head a little as though to clear it, and he said gruffly, "You did a good job. We should thank you. I mentioned your work in my report."

"Thank you, sir," said Corell. "I did my best."

Lanser said, a little wearily, "Well, sir, now what shall we do? Would you like to go back to the capital? We can put you on a coal barge if you're in a hurry, or on a destroyer if you want to wait."

Corell said, "But I don't want to go back. I'll stay here."

Lanser studied this for a moment and he said, "You know, I haven't a great many men. I can't give you a very adequate bodyguard."

"But I don't need a bodyguard. I tell you these aren't violent people."

Lanser looked at the bandage for a moment. Hunter glanced up from his board and remarked, "You'd better start wearing a helmet." He looked down at his work again.

Now Corell moved forward in his chair. "I wanted particularly to talk to you, Colonel. I thought I might help with the civil administration."

Lanser turned on his heel and walked to the window and looked out, and then he swung around and said quietly, "What have you in mind?"

"Well, you must have a civil authority you can trust. I thought perhaps that Mayor Orden might step down now and—well, if I were to take over his office, it and the military would work very nicely together."

Lanser's eyes seemed to grow large and bright. He came close to Corell and he spoke sharply. "Have you mentioned this in your report?"

Corell said, "Well, yes, naturally—in my analysis."

Lanser interrupted. "Have you talked to any of the town people since we arrived—outside of the Mayor, that is?"

"Well, no. You see, they are still a bit startled. They didn't expect it." He chuckled. "No, sir, they certainly didn't expect it."

But Lanser pressed his point. "So you don't really know what's going on in their minds?"

"Why, they're startled," said Corell. "They're—well, they're almost dreaming."

"You don't know what they think of you?" Lanser asked.

"I have many friends here. I know everyone."

"Did anyone buy anything in your store this morning?"

"Well, of course, business is at a standstill," Corell answered. "No one's buying anything."

Lanser relaxed suddenly. He went to a chair and sat down and crossed his legs. He said quietly, "Yours is a difficult and brave branch of the service. It should be greatly rewarded."

"Thank you, sir."

"You will have their hatred in time," said the colonel.

"I can stand that, sir. They are the enemy."

Now Lanser hesitated a long moment before he spoke, and then he said softly, "You will not even have *our* respect."

Corell jumped to his feet excitedly. "This is contrary to the Leader's words!" he said. "The Leader has said that all branches are equally honorable."

Lanser went on very quietly, "I hope the Leader knows. I hope he can read the minds of soldiers." And then almost compassionately he said, "You should be greatly rewarded." For a moment he sat quietly and then he pulled himself together and said, "Now we must come to exactness. I am in charge here. My job is to get coal out. To do that I must maintain order and discipline, and to do that I must know what is in the minds of these people. I must anticipate revolt. Do you understand that?"

"Well, I can find out what you wish to know, sir. As Mayor here, I will be very effective," said Corell.

Lanser shook his head. "I have no orders about this. I must use my own judgment. I think you will never again know what is going on here. I think no one will speak to you; no one will be near to you except those people who will live on money, who can live on money. I think without a guard you will be in great danger. It will please me if you go back to the capital, there to be rewarded for your fine work."

"But my place is here, sir," said Corell. "I have made my place. It is all in my report."

Lanser went on as though he had not heard. "Mayor Orden is more than a mayor," he said. "He is his people. He knows what they are doing, thinking, without asking, because he will think what they think. By watching him I will know them. He must stay. That is my judgment."

Corell said, "My work, sir, merits better treatment than being sent away."

"Yes, it does," Lanser said slowly. "But to the larger work I think you are only a detriment now. If you are not hated yet, you will be. In any little revolt you will

[65]

be the first to be killed. I think I will suggest that you go back."

Corell said stiffly, "You will, of course, permit me to wait for a reply to my report to the capital?"

"Yes, of course. But I shall recommend that you go back for your own safety. Frankly, Mr. Corell, you have no value here. But—well, there must be other plans and other countries. Perhaps you will go now to some new town in some new country. You will win new confidence in a new field. You may be given a larger town, even a city, a greater responsibility. I think I will recommend you highly for your work here."

Corell's eyes were shining with gratification. "Thank you, sir," he said. "I've worked hard. Perhaps you are right. But you must permit me to wait for the reply from the capital."

Lanser's voice was tight. His eyes were slitted. He said harshly, "Wear a helmet, keep indoors, do not go out at night, and, above all, do not drink. Trust no woman nor any man. Do you understand that?"

Corell looked pityingly at the colonel. "I don't think you understand. I have a little house. A pleasant country girl waits on me. I even think she's a little fond of me. These are simple, peaceful people. I know them."

Lanser said, "There are no peaceful people. When will you learn it? There are no friendly people. Can't you understand that? We have invaded this country—you, by what they call treachery, prepared for us." His face grew red and his voice rose. "Can't you understand that we are at war with these people?"

Corell said, a little smugly, "We have defeated them."

The colonel stood up and swung his arms helplessly, and Hunter looked up from his board and put his hand out to protect his board from being jiggled. Hunter said, "Careful now, sir. I'm inking in. I wouldn't want to do it all over again."

Lanser looked down at him and said, "Sorry," and went on as though he were instructing a class. He said, "Defeat is a momentary thing. A defeat doesn't last. We were defeated and now we attack. Defeat means nothing. Can't you understand that? Do you know what they are whispering behind doors?"

Corell asked, "Do you?"

"No, but I suspect."

Then Corell said insinuatingly, "Are you afraid, Colonel? Should the commander of this occupation be afraid?"

Lanser sat down heavily and said, "Maybe that's it." And he said disgustedly, "I'm tired of people who have not been at war who know all about it." He held his chin in his hand and said, "I remember a little old woman in Brussels—sweet face, white hair; she was only four feet eleven; delicate old hands. You could see the veins almost black against her skin. And her black shawl and her blue-white hair. She used to sing our national songs to us in a quivering, sweet voice. She always knew where to find a cigarette or a virgin." He dropped his hand from his chin, and he caught himself as though he had been asleep. "We didn't know her son had been executed," he said. "When we finally shot her, she had killed twelve men with a long, black hatpin. I have it yet at home. It has an enamel button with a bird over it, red and blue."

Corell said, "But you shot her?"

"Of course we shot her."

"And the murders stopped?" asked Corell.

"No, the murders did not stop. And when we finally retreated, the people cut off stragglers and they burned some and they gouged the eyes from some, and some they even crucified."

Corell said loudly, "These are not good things to say, Colonel."

"They are not good things to remember," said Lanser.

Corell said, "You should not be in command if you are afraid."

And Lanser answered softly, "I know how to fight, you see. If you know, at least you do not make silly errors."

"Do you talk this way to the young officers?"

Lanser shook his head. "No, they wouldn't believe me."

"Why do you tell me, then?"

"Because, Mr. Corell, your work is done. I remember one time—" and as he spoke there was a tumble of feet on the stairs and the door burst open. A sentry looked in and Captain Loft brushed past him. Loft was rigid and cold and military; he said, "There's trouble, sir."

"Trouble?"

"I have to report, sir, that Captain Bentick has been killed."

Lanser said, "Oh—yes—Bentick!"

There was the sound of a number of footsteps on the stairs and two stretcher-bearers came in, carrying a figure covered with blankets.

Lanser said, "Are you sure he's dead?"

"Quite sure," Loft said stiffly.

The lieutenants came in from the bedroom, their mouths a little open, and they looked frightened. Lanser said, "Put him down there," and he pointed to the wall beside the windows. When the bearers had gone, Lanser knelt and lifted a corner of the blanket and then quickly put it down again. And still kneeling, he looked at Loft and said, "Who did this?"

"A miner," said Loft.

"Why?"

"I was there, sir."

"Well, make your report, then! Make your report, damn it, man!"

Loft drew himself up and said formally, "I had just relieved Captain Bentick, as the colonel ordered. Captain Bentick was about to leave to come here when I had some trouble about a recalcitrant miner who wanted to quit work. He shouted something about being a free man. When I ordered him to work, he rushed at me with his pick. Captain Bentick tried to interfere." He gestured slightly toward the body.

Lanser, still kneeling, nodded slowly. "Bentick was a curious man," he said. "He loved the English. He loved everything about them. I don't think he liked to fight very much. . . . You captured the man?"

"Yes, sir," Loft said.

Lanser stood up slowly and spoke as though to himself. "So it starts again. We will shoot this man and make twenty new enemies. It's the only thing we know, the only thing we know."

Prackle said, "What do you say, sir?"

Lanser answered, "Nothing, nothing at all. I was just thinking." He turned to Loft and said, "Please give my compliments to Mayor Orden and my request that he see me immediately. It is very important."

Major Hunter looked up, dried his inking-pen carefully, and put it away in a velvet-lined box.

CHAPTER THREE

In the town the people moved sullenly through the streets. Some of the light of astonishment was gone from their eyes, but still a light of anger had not taken its place. In the coal shaft the workingmen pushed the coal cars sullenly. The small tradesmen stood behind their counters and served the people, but no one communicated with them. The people spoke to one another in monosyllables, and everyone was thinking of the war, thinking of himself, thinking of the past and how it had suddenly been changed.

In the drawing-room of the palace of Mayor Orden a small fire burned and the lights were on, for it was a gray day outside and there was frost in the air. The room was itself undergoing a change. The tapestry-covered chairs were pushed back, the little tables out of the way, and through the doorway to the right Joseph and Annie were struggling to bring in a large, square dining-table. They had it on its side. Joseph was in the drawing-room and Annie's red face showed through the door. Joseph maneuvered the legs around sideways, and he cried, "Don't push, Annie! Now!"

"I am 'now-ing,'" said Annie the red-nosed, the red-eyed, the angry. Annie was always a little angry and these soldiers, this occupation, did not improve her temper. Indeed, what for years had been considered simply a bad disposition was suddenly become a patriotic emotion. Annie had gained some little reputation as an exponent of liberty by throwing hot water on the soldiers. She would have thrown it on anyone who cluttered up her porch, but it just happened that she had become a heroine; and since anger had been the beginning of her success, Annie went on to new successes by whipping herself into increased and constant anger.

"Don't scuff the bottom," Joseph said. The table wedged in the doorway. "Steady!" Joseph warned.

"I am steady," said Annie.

Joseph stood off and studied the table, and Annie crossed her arms and glared at him. He tested a leg. "Don't push," he said. "Don't push so hard." And by himself he got the table through while Annie followed with crossed arms. "Now, up she goes," said Joseph, and at last Annie helped him settle it on four legs and move it to the center of the room. "There," Annie said. "If His Excellency hadn't told me to, I wouldn't have done it. What right have they got moving tables around?"

"What right coming in at all?" said Joseph.

"None," said Annie.

"None," repeated Joseph. "I see it like they have no right at all, but they do it, with their guns and their parachutes; they do it, Annie."

"They got no right," said Annie. "What do they want with a table in here, anyway? This isn't a dining-room."

Joseph moved a chair up to the table and he set it carefully at the right distance from the table, and he adjusted it. "They're going to hold a trial," he said. "They're going to try Alexander Morden."

"Molly Morden's husband?"

[74]

"Molly Morden's husband."

"For bashing that fellow with a pick?"

"That's right," said Joseph.

"But he's a nice man," Annie said. "They've got no right to try him. He gave Molly a big red dress for her birthday. What right have they got to try Alex?"

"Well," Joseph explained, "he killed this fellow."

"Suppose he did; the fellow ordered Alex around. I heard about it. Alex doesn't like to be ordered. Alex's been an alderman in his time, and his father, too. And Molly Morden makes a nice cake," Annie said charitably. "But her frosting gets too hard. What'll they do with Alex?"

"Shoot him," Joseph said gloomily.

"They can't do that."

"Bring up the chairs, Annie. Yes, they can. They'll just do it."

Annie shook a very rigid finger in his face. "You remember my words," she said angrily. "People aren't going to like it if they hurt Alex. People like Alex. Did he ever hurt anybody before? Answer me that!"

"No," said Joseph.

"Well, there, you see! If they hurt Alex, people are going to be mad and I'm going to be mad. I won't stand for it!"

"What will you do?" Joseph asked her.

"Why, I'll kill some of them myself," said Annie.

"And then they'll shoot you," said Joseph.

"Let them! I tell you, Joseph, things can go too far —tramping in and out all hours of the night, shooting people."

Joseph adjusted a chair at the head of the table, and he became in some curious way a conspirator. He said softly, "Annie."

She paused and, sensing his tone, walked nearer to him. He said, "Can you keep a secret?"

She looked at him with a little admiration, for he had never had a secret before. "Yes. What is it?"

"Well, William Deal and Walter Doggel got away last night."

"Got away? Where?"

"They got away to England, in a boat."

Annie sighed with pleasure and anticipation. "Does everybody know it?"

"Well, not everybody," said Joseph. "Everybody

but—" and he pointed a quick thumb toward the ceiling.

"When did they go? Why didn't I hear about it?"

"You were busy." Joseph's voice and face were cold. "You know that Corell?"

"Yes."

Joseph came close to her. "I don't think he's going to live long."

"What do you mean?" Annie asked.

"Well, people are talking."

Annie sighed with tension. "Ah-h-h!!"

Joseph at last had opinions. "People are getting together," he said. "They don't like to be conquered. Things are going to happen. You keep your eyes peeled, Annie. There're going to be things for you to do."

Annie asked, "How about His Excellency? What's he going to do? How does His Excellency stand?"

"Nobody knows," said Joseph. "He doesn't say anything."

"He wouldn't be against us," Annie said.

"He doesn't say," said Joseph.

The knob turned on the left-hand door, and Mayor

Orden came in slowly. He looked tired and old. Behind him Doctor Winter walked. Orden said, "That's good, Joseph. Thank you, Annie. It looks very well."

They went out and Joseph looked back through the door for a moment before he closed it.

Mayor Orden walked to the fire and turned to warm his back. Doctor Winter pulled out the chair at the head of the table and sat down. "I wonder how much longer I can hold this position?" Orden said. "The people don't quite trust me and neither does the enemy. I wonder whether this is a good thing."

"I don't know," said Winter. "You trust yourself, don't you? There's no doubt in your own mind?"

"Doubt? No. I am the Mayor. I don't understand many things." He pointed to the table. "I don't know why they have to hold this trial in here. They're going to try Alex Morden here for murder. You remember Alex? He has that pretty little wife, Molly."

"I remember," said Winter. "She used to teach in the grammar school. Yes, I remember. She's so pretty, she hated to get glasses when she needed them. Well, I guess Alex killed an officer, all right. Nobody's questioned that."

Mayor Orden said bitterly, "Nobody questions it. But why do they try him? Why don't they shoot him? This is not a matter of doubt or certainty, justice or injustice. There's none of that here. Why must they try him—and in my house?"

Winter said, "I would guess it is for the show. There's an idea about it: if you go through the form of a thing, you have it, and sometimes people are satisfied with the form of a thing. We had an army—soldiers with guns—but it wasn't an army, you see. The invaders will have a trial and hope to convince the people that there is justice involved. Alex did kill the captain, you know."

"Yes, I see that," Orden said.

And Winter went on, "If it comes from your house, where the people expect justice——"

He was interrupted by the opening of the door to the right. A young woman entered. She was about thirty and quite pretty. She carried her glasses in her hand. She was dressed simply and neatly and she was very excited. She said quickly, "Annie told me to come right in, sir."

"Why, of course," said the Mayor. "You're Molly Morden."

"Yes, sir; I am. They say that Alex is to be tried and shot."

Orden looked down at the floor for a moment, and Molly went on, "They say you will sentence him. It will be your words that send him out."

Orden looked up, startled. "What's this? Who says this?"

"The people in the town." She held herself very straight and she asked, half pleadingly, half demandingly, "You wouldn't do that, would you, sir?"

"How could the people know what I don't know?" he said.

"That is a great mystery," said Doctor Winter. "That is a mystery that has disturbed rulers all over the world—how the people know. It disturbs the invaders now, I am told, how news runs through censorships, how the truth of things fights free of control. It is a great mystery."

The girl looked up, for the room had suddenly darkened, and she seemed to be afraid. "It's a cloud," she said. "There's word snow is on the way, and it's early, too." Doctor Winter went to the window and squinted up at the sky, and he said, "Yes, it's a big cloud; maybe it will pass over."

Mayor Orden switched on a lamp that made only a little circle of light. He switched it off again and said, "A light in the daytime is a lonely thing."

Now Molly came near to him again. "Alex is not a murdering man," she said. "He's a quick-tempered man, but he's never broken a law. He's a respected man."

Orden rested his hand on her shoulder and he said, "I have known Alex since he was a little boy. I knew his father and his grandfather. His grandfather was a bear-hunter in the old days. Did you know that?"

Molly ignored him. "You wouldn't sentence Alex?"

"No," he said. "How could I sentence him?"

"The people said you would, for the sake of order."

Mayor Orden stood behind a chair and gripped its back with his hands. "Do the people want order, Molly?"

"I don't know," she said. "They want to be free."

"Well, do they know how to go about it? Do they know what method to use against an armed enemy?"

"No," Molly said, "I don't think so."

"You are a bright girl, Molly; do you know?"

"No, sir, but I think the people feel that they are beaten if they are docile. They want to show these soldiers they're unbeaten."

"They've had no chance to fight. It's no fight to go against machine guns," Doctor Winter said.

Orden said, "When you know what they want to do, will you tell me, Molly?"

She looked at him suspiciously. "Yes—" she said.

"You mean 'no.' You don't trust me."

"But how about Alex?" she questioned.

"I'll not sentence him. He has committed no crime against our people," said the Mayor.

Molly was hesitant now. She said, "Will they—will they kill Alex?"

Orden stared at her and he said, "Dear child, my dear child."

She held herself rigid. "Thank you."

Orden came close to her and she said weakly, "Don't touch me. Please don't touch me. Please don't touch me." And his hand dropped. For a moment she stood still, then she turned stiffly and went out of the door.

She had just closed the door when Joseph entered. "Excuse me, sir, the colonel wants to see you. I said you were busy. I knew she was here. And Madame wants to see you, too."

Orden said, "Ask Madame to come in."

Joseph went out and Madame came in immediately.

"I don't know how I can run a house," she began; "it's more people than the house can stand. Annie's angry all the time."

"Hush!" Orden said.

Madame looked at him in amazement. "I don't know what——"

"Hush!" he said. "Sarah, I want you to go to Alex Morden's house. Do you understand? I want you to stay with Molly Morden while she needs you. Don't talk, just stay with her."

Madame said, "I've a hundred things——"

"Sarah, I want you to stay with Molly Morden. Don't leave her alone. Go now."

She comprehended slowly. "Yes," she said. "Yes, I will. When will it be over?"

"I don't know," he said. "I'll send Annie when it's time."

She kissed him lightly on the cheek and went out. Orden walked to the door and called, "Joseph, I'll see the colonel now."

Lanser came in. He had on a new pressed uniform with a little ornamental dagger at the belt. He said, "Good morning, Your Excellency. I wish to speak to you informally." He glanced at Doctor Winter. "I should like to speak to you alone."

Winter went slowly to the door and as he reached it Orden said, "Doctor!"

Winter turned. "Yes?"

"Will you come back this evening?"

"You will have work for me?" the doctor asked.

"No—no. I just won't like to be alone."

"I will be here," said the doctor.

"And, Doctor, do you think Molly looked all right?"

"Oh, I think so. Close to hysteria, I guess. But she's good stock. She's good, strong stock. She is a Kenderly, you know."

"I'd forgotten," Orden said. "Yes, she is a Kenderly, isn't she?"

Doctor Winter went out and shut the door gently behind him.

Lanser had waited courteously. He watched the door close. He looked at the table and the chairs about it. "I will not tell you, sir, how sorry I am about this. I wish it had not happened."

Mayor Orden bowed, and Lanser went on, "I like you, sir, and I respect you, but I have a job to do. You surely recognize that."

Orden did not answer. He looked straight into Lanser's eyes.

"We do not act alone or on our own judgment."

Between sentences Lanser waited for an answer but he received none.

"There are rules laid down for us, rules made in the capital. This man has killed an officer."

At last Orden answered, "Why didn't you shoot him then? That was the time to do it."

Lanser shook his head. "If I agreed with you, it would make no difference. You know as well as I that punishment is largely for the purpose of deterring the potential criminal. Thus, since punishment is for others than the punished, it must be publicized. It must even be dramatized." He thrust a finger in back of his belt and flipped his little dagger.

Orden turned away and looked out of the window at the dark sky. "It will snow tonight," he said.

"Mayor Orden, you know our orders are inexorable. We must get the coal. If your people are not orderly, we will have to restore that order by force." His voice grew stern. "We must shoot people if it is necessary. If you wish to save your people from hurt, you must help us to keep order. Now, it is considered wise by my government that punishment emanate from the local authority. It makes for a more orderly situation."

Orden said softly, "So the people did know. That is a mystery." And louder he said, "You wish me to pass sentence of death on Alexander Morden after a trial here?"

"Yes, and you will prevent much bloodshed later if you will do it."

Orden went to the table and pulled out the big chair at its head and sat down. And suddenly he seemed to be the judge, with Lanser the culprit. He drummed with his fingers on the table. He said, "You and your government do not understand. In all the world yours is the only government and people with a record of defeat after defeat for centuries and every time because you did not understand people." He paused. "This principle does not work. First, I am the Mayor. I have no right to pass sentence of death. There is no one in this community with that right. If I should do it, I would be breaking the law as much as you."

"Breaking the law?" said Lanser.

"You killed six men when you came in. Under our law you are guilty of murder, all of you. Why do you go into this nonsense of law, Colonel? There is no law between you and us. This is war. Don't you know you will have to kill all of us or we in time will kill all of you? You destroyed the law when you came in, and a new law took its place. Don't you know that?"

Lanser said, "May I sit down?"

"Why do you ask? That is another lie. You could make me stand if you wished."

Lanser said, "No; it is true whether you believe it or not: personally, I have respect for you and your office, and"—he put his forehead in his hand for a moment—"you see, what I think, sir, I, a man of a certain age and certain memories, is of no importance. I might agree

[87]

with you, but that would change nothing. The military, the political pattern I work in has certain tendencies and practices which are invariable."

Orden said, "And these tendencies and practices have been proven wrong in every single case since the beginning of the world."

Lanser laughed bitterly. "I, an individual man with certain memories, might agree with you, might even add that one of the tendencies of the military mind and pattern is an inability to learn, an inability to see beyond the killing which is its job. But I am not a man subject to memories. The coal miner must be shot publicly, because the theory is that others will then restrain themselves from killing our men."

Orden said, "We need not talk any more, then."

"Yes, we must talk. We want you to help."

Orden sat quietly for a while and then he said, "I'll tell you what I'll do. How many men were on the machine guns which killed our soldiers?"

"Oh, not more than twenty, I guess," said Lanser.

"Very well. If you will shoot them, I will condemn Morden."

"You're not serious!" said the colonel.

"But I am serious."

"This can't be done. You know it."

"I know it," said Orden. "And what you ask cannot be done."

Lanser said, "I suppose I knew. Corell will have to be Mayor after all." He looked up quickly. "You will stay for the trial?"

"Yes, I'll stay. Then Alex won't be so lonely."

Lanser looked at him and smiled a little sadly. "We have taken on a job, haven't we?"

"Yes," said the Mayor, "the one impossible job in the world, the one thing that can't be done."

"And that is?"

"To break man's spirit permanently."

Orden's head sank a little toward the table, and he said, without looking up, "It's started to snow. It didn't wait for night. I like the sweet, cool smell of the snow."

CHAPTER FOUR

BY ELEVEN O'CLOCK the snow was falling
heavily in big, soft puffs and the sky was not visible
at all. People were scurrying through the falling snow,
and snow piled up in the doorways and it piled up on
the statue in the public square and on the rails from
the mine to the harbor. Snow piled up and the little
cartwheels skidded as they were pushed along. And
over the town there hung a blackness that was deeper
than the cloud, and over the town there hung a sullen-
ness and a dry, growing hatred. The people did not
stand in the streets long, but they entered the doors
and the doors closed and there seemed to be eyes looking from behind the curtains, and when the military
went through the street or when the patrol walked

down the main street, the eyes were on the patrol, cold and sullen. And in the shops people came to buy little things for lunch and they asked for the goods and got it and paid for it and exchanged no good-day with the seller.

In the little palace drawing-room the lights were on and the lights shone on the falling snow outside the window. The court was in session. Lanser sat at the head of the table with Hunter on his right, then Tonder, and, at the lower end, Captain Loft with a little pile of papers in front of him. On the opposite side, Mayor Orden sat on the colonel's left and Prackle was next to him—Prackle, who scribbled on his pad of paper. Beside the table two guards stood with bayonets fixed, with helmets on their heads, and they were little wooden images. Between them was Alex Morden, a big young man with a wide, low forehead, with deep-set eyes and a long, sharp nose. His chin was firm and his mouth sensual and wide. He was wide of shoulder, narrow of hip, and in front of him his man-acled hands clasped and unclasped. He was dressed in black trousers, a blue shirt open at the neck, and a dark coat shiny from wear.

Captain Loft read from the paper in front of him, " 'When ordered back to work, he refused to go, and when the order was repeated, the prisoner attacked Captain Loft with the pick-ax he carried. Captain Bentick interposed his body——' "

Mayor Orden coughed and, when Loft stopped reading, said, "Sit down, Alex. One of you guards get him a chair." The guard turned and pulled up a chair unquestioningly.

Loft said, "It is customary for the prisoner to stand."

"Let him sit down," Orden said. "Only we will know. You can report that he stood."

"It is not customary to falsify reports," said Loft.

"Sit down, Alex," Orden repeated.

And the big young man sat down and his manacled hands were restless in his lap.

Loft began, "This is contrary to all——"

The colonel said, "Let him be seated."

Captain Loft cleared his throat. " 'Captain Bentick interposed his body and received a blow on the head which crushed his skull.' A medical report is appended. Do you wish me to read it?"

"No need," said Lanser. "Make it as quick as you can."

" 'These facts have been witnessed by several of our soldiers, whose statements are attached. This military court finds that the prisoner is guilty of murder and recommends a death sentence.' Do you wish me to read the statements of the soldiers?"

Lanser sighed. "No." He turned to Alex. "You don't deny that you killed the captain, do you?"

Alex smiled sadly. "I hit him," he said. "I don't know that I killed him."

Orden said, "Good work, Alex!" And the two looked at each other as friends.

Loft said, "Do you mean to imply that he was killed by someone else?"

"I don't know," said Alex. "I only hit him, and then somebody hit me."

Colonel Lanser said, "Do you want to offer any explanation? I can't think of anything that will change the sentence, but we will listen."

Loft said, "I respectfully submit that the colonel should not have said that. It indicates that the court is not impartial."

Orden laughed dryly. The colonel looked at him and smiled a little. "Have you any explanation?" he repeated.

Alex lifted a hand to gesture and the other came with it. He looked embarrassed and put them in his lap again. "I was mad," he said. "I have a pretty bad temper. He said I must work. I am a free man. I got mad and I hit him. I guess I hit him hard. It was the wrong man." He pointed at Loft. "That's the man I wanted to hit, that one."

Lanser said, "It doesn't matter whom you wanted to hit. Anybody would have been the same. Are you sorry you did it?" He said aside to the table, "It would look well in the record if he were sorry."

"Sorry?" Alex asked. "I'm not sorry. He told me to go to work—me, a free man! I used to be alderman. He said I had to work."

"But if the sentence is death, won't you be sorry then?"

Alex sank his head and really tried to think honestly. "No," he said. "You mean, would I do it again?"

"That's what I mean."

"No," Alex said thoughtfully, "I don't think I'm sorry."

Lanser said, "Put in the record that the prisoner was overcome with remorse. Sentence is automatic. Do you understand?" he said to Alex. "The court has no leeway. The court finds you guilty and sentences you to be shot immediately. I do not see any reason to torture you with this any more. Captain Loft, is there anything I have forgotten?"

"You've forgotten me," said Orden. He stood up and pushed back his chair and stepped over to Alex. And Alex, from long habit, stood up respectfully. "Alexander, I am the elected Mayor."

"I know it, sir."

"Alex, these men are invaders. They have taken our country by surprise and treachery and force."

Captain Loft said, "Sir, this should not be permitted."

Lanser said, "Hush! Is it better to hear it, or would you rather it were whispered?"

Orden went on as though he had not been interrupted. "When they came, the people were confused and I was confused. We did not know what to do or think. Yours was the first clear act. Your private anger was the beginning of a public anger. I know it is said in town that I am acting with these men. I can show the town, but you—you are going to die. I want you to know."

Alex dropped his head and then raised it. "I know, sir."

Lanser said, "Is the squad ready?"

"Outside, sir."

"Who is commanding?"

"Lieutenant Tonder, sir."

Tonder raised his head and his chin was hard and he held his breath.

Orden said softly, "Are you afraid, Alex?"

And Alex said, "Yes, sir."

"I can't tell you not to be. I would be, too, and so would these young—gods of war."

Lanser said, "Call your squad." Tonder got up quickly and went to the door. "They're here, sir." He opened the door wide and the helmeted men could be seen.

Orden said, "Alex, go, knowing that these men will have no rest, no rest at all until they are gone, or dead. You will make the people one. It's a sad knowledge and little enough gift to you, but it is so. No rest at all."

Alex shut his eyes tightly. Mayor Orden leaned close and kissed him on the cheek. "Good-by, Alex," he said.

The guard took Alex by the arm and the young man kept his eyes tightly closed, and they guided him through the door. The squad faced about, and their feet marched away down out of the house and into the snow, and the snow muffled their footsteps.

The men about the table were silent. Orden looked toward the window and saw a little round spot being rubbed clear of snow by a quick hand. He stared at it, fascinated, and then he looked quickly away. He said to the colonel, "I hope you know what you are doing."

Captain Loft gathered his papers and Lanser asked, "In the square, Captain?"

"Yes, in the square. It must be public," Loft said.

And Orden said, "I hope you know."

"Man," said the colonel, "whether we know or not, it is what must be done."

Silence fell on the room and each man listened. And it was not long. From the distance there came a crash of firing. Lanser sighed deeply. Orden put his hand to his forehead and filled his lungs deeply. Then there was a shout outside. The glass of the window crashed inward and Lieutenant Prackle wheeled about. He brought his hand up to his shoulder and stared at it.

Lanser leaped up, crying, "So, it starts! Are you badly hurt, Lieutenant?"

"My shoulder," said Prackle.

Lanser took command. "Captain Loft, there will be tracks in the snow. Now, I want every house searched for firearms. I want every man who has one taken hostage. You, sir," he said to the Mayor, "are placed in protective custody. And understand this, please: we will shoot, five, ten, a hundred for one."

Orden said quietly, "A man of certain memories."

Lanser stopped in the middle of an order. He looked over slowly at the Mayor and for a moment they understood each other. And then Lanser straightened his shoulders. "A man of no memories!" he said sharply. And then, "I want every weapon in town gathered.

Bring in everyone who resists. Hurry, before their tracks are filled."

The staff found their helmets and loosed their pistols and started out. And Orden went to the broken window. He said sadly, "The sweet, cool smell of the snow."

CHAPTER FIVE

THE DAYS and the weeks dragged on, and the months dragged on. The snow fell and melted and fell and melted and finally fell and stuck. The dark buildings of the little town wore bells and hats and eyebrows of white and there were trenches through the snow to the doorways. In the harbor the coal barges came empty and went away loaded, but the coal did not come out of the ground easily. The good miners made mistakes. They were clumsy and slow. Machinery broke and took a long time to fix. The people of the conquered country settled in a slow, silent, waiting revenge. The men who had been traitors, who had helped the invaders—and many of them believed it was for a better state and an ideal way of life—found that the control they took was insecure, that the people they had known looked at them coldly and never spoke.

And there was death in the air, hovering and waiting. Accidents happened on the railroad, which clung to the mountains and connected the little town with the rest of the nation. Avalanches poured down on the tracks and rails were spread. No train could move unless the tracks were first inspected. People were shot in reprisal and it made no difference. Now and then a group of young men escaped and went to England. And the English bombed the coal mine and did some damage and killed some of both their friends and their enemies. And it did no good. The cold hatred grew with the winter, the silent, sullen hatred, the waiting hatred. The food supply was controlled—issued to the obedient and withheld from the disobedient—so that the whole population turned coldly obedient. There was a point where food could not be withheld, for a starving man cannot mine coal, cannot lift and carry. And the hatred was deep in the eyes of the people, beneath the surface.

Now it was that the conqueror was surrounded, the

men of the battalion alone among silent enemies, and no man might relax his guard for even a moment. If he did, he disappeared, and some snowdrift received his body. If he went alone to a woman, he disappeared and some snowdrift received his body. If he drank, he disappeared. The men of the battalion could sing only together, could dance only together, and dancing gradually stopped and the singing expressed a longing for home. Their talk was of friends and relatives who loved them and their longings were for warmth and love, because a man can be a soldier for only so many hours a day and for only so many months in a year, and then he wants to be a man again, wants girls and drinks and music and laughter and ease, and when these are cut off, they become irresistibly desirable.

And the men thought always of home. The men of the battalion came to detest the place they had conquered, and they were curt with the people and the people were curt with them, and gradually a little fear began to grow in the conquerors, a fear that it would never be over, that they could never relax or go home, a fear that one day they would crack and be hunted through the mountains like rabbits, for the conquered never relaxed their hatred. The patrols, seeing lights, hearing laughter, would be drawn as to a fire, and when they came near, the laughter stopped, the warmth went out, and the people were cold and obedient. And the soldiers, smelling warm food from the little restaurants, went in and ordered the warm food and found that it was oversalted or overpeppered.

Then the soldiers read the news from home and from the other conquered countries, and the news was always good, and for a little while they believed it, and then after a while they did not believe it any more. And every man carried in his heart the terror. "If home crumbled, they would not tell us, and then it would be too late. These people will not spare us. They will kill us all." They remembered stories of their men retreating through Belgium and retreating out of Russia. And the more literate remembered the frantic, tragic retreat from Moscow, when every peasant's pitchfork tasted blood and the snow was rotten with bodies.

And they knew when they cracked, or relaxed, or slept too long, it would be the same here, and their sleep was restless and their days were nervous. They asked questions their officers could not answer because they did not know. They were not told, either. They did not believe the reports from home, either.

Thus it came about that the conquerors grew afraid of the conquered and their nerves wore thin and they shot at shadows in the night. The cold, sullen silence was with them always. Then three soldiers went insane in a week and cried all night and all day until they were sent away home. And others might have gone insane if they had not heard that mercy deaths awaited the insane at home, and a mercy death is a terrible thing to think of. Fear crept in on the men in their billets and it made them sad, and it crept into the patrols and it made them cruel.

The year turned and the nights grew long. It was dark at three o'clock in the afternoon and not light again until nine in the morning. The jolly lights did not shine out on the snow, for by law every window must be black against the bombers. And yet when the English bombers came over, some light always appeared near the coal mine. Sometimes the sentries shot a man with a lantern and once a girl with a flashlight.

And it did no good. Nothing was cured by the shooting.

And the officers were a reflection of their men, more restrained because their training was more complete, more resourceful because they had more responsibility, but the same fears were a little deeper buried in them, the same longings were more tightly locked in their hearts. And they were under a double strain, for the conquered people watched them for mistakes and their own men watched them for weakness, so that their spirits were taut to the breaking-point. The conquerors were under a terrible spiritual siege and everyone knew, conquered and conquerors, what would happen when the first crack appeared.

From the upstairs room of the Mayor's palace the comfort seemed to have gone. Over the windows black paper was tacked tightly and there were little piles of precious equipment about the room—the instruments and equipment that could not be jeopardized, the glasses and masks and helmets. And discipline here at least was laxer, as though these officers knew there must be some laxness somewhere or the machine would break. On the table were two gasoline lanterns which threw a hard, brilliant light and they made great shadows on the walls, and their hissing was an undercurrent in the room.

Major Hunter went on with his work. His drawing-board was permanently ready now, for the bombs tore out his work nearly as fast as he put it in. And he had little sorrow, for to Major Hunter building was life and here he had more building than he could project or accomplish. He sat at his drawing-board with a light behind him and his T-square moved up and down the board and his pencil was busy.

Lieutenant Prackle, his arm still in a sling, sat in a straight chair behind the center table, reading an illustrated paper. At the end of the table Lieutenant Tonder was writing a letter. He held his pen pinched high and occasionally he looked up from his letter and gazed at the ceiling, to find words to put in his letter.

Prackle turned a page of the illustrated paper and he said, "I can close my eyes and see every shop on this street here." And Hunter went on with his work and Tonder wrote a few more words. Prackle continued, "There is a restaurant right behind here. You can't see it in the picture. It's called Burden's."

Hunter did not look up. He said, "I know the place. They had good scallops."

"Sure they did," Prackle said. "Everything was good there. Not a single bad thing did they serve. And their coffee——"

Tonder looked up from his letter and said, "They won't be serving coffee now—or scallops."

"Well, I don't know about that," said Prackle. "They did and they will again. And there was a waitress there." He described her figure with his hand, with the good hand. "Blonde, so and so." He looked down at the magazine. "She had the strangest eyes—has, I mean —always kind of moist-looking as though she had just been laughing or crying." He glanced at the ceiling and he spoke softly. "I was out with her. She was lovely. I wonder why I didn't go back oftener. I wonder if she's still there."

Tonder said gloomily, "Probably not. Working in a factory, maybe."

Prackle laughed. "I hope they aren't rationing girls at home."

"Why not?" said Tonder.

Prackle said playfully, "You don't care much for girls, do you? Not much, you don't!"

Tonder said, "I like them for what girls are for. I don't let them crawl around my other life."

And Prackle said tauntingly, "It seems to me that they crawl all over you all the time."

Tonder tried to change the subject. He said, "I hate these damn lanterns. Major, when are you going to get that dynamo fixed?"

Major Hunter looked up slowly from his board and said, "It should be done by now. I've got good men working on it. I'll double the guard on it from now on, I guess."

"Did you get the fellow that wrecked it?" Prackle asked.

And Hunter said grimly, "It might be any one of five men. I got all five." He went on musingly, "It's so easy to wreck a dynamo if you know how. Just short it and it wrecks itself." He said, "The light ought to be on any time now."

Prackle still looked at his magazine. "I wonder when we will be relieved. I wonder when we will go home for a while. Major, wouldn't you like to go home for a rest?"

Hunter looked up from his work and his face was hopeless for a moment. "Yes, of course." He recovered himself. "I've built this siding four times. I don't know why a bomb always knocks out this particular siding. I'm getting tired of this piece of track. I have to change the route every time because of the craters. There's no time to fill them in. The ground is frozen too hard. It seems to be too much work."

Suddenly the electric lights came on and Tonder automatically reached out and turned off the two gasoline lanterns. The hissing was gone from the room.

Tonder said, "Thank God for that! That hissing gets on my nerves. It makes me think there's whispering." He folded the letter he had been writing and he said, "It's strange more letters don't come through. I've only had one in two weeks."

Prackle said, "Maybe nobody writes to you."

"Maybe," said Tonder. He turned to the major. "If anything happened—at home, I mean—do you think they would let us know—anything bad, I mean, any deaths or anything like that?"

Hunter said, "I don't know."

"Well," Tonder went on, "I would like to get out of this god-forsaken hole!"

Prackle broke in, "I thought you were going to live here after the war?" And he imitated Tonder's voice. "Put four or five farms together. Make a nice place, a kind of family seat. Wasn't that it? Going to be a little lord of the valley, weren't you? Nice, pleasant people, beautiful lawns and deer and little children. Isn't that the way it was, Tonder?"

As Prackle spoke, Tonder's hand dropped. Then he clasped his temples with his hands and he spoke with emotion. "Be still! Don't talk like that! These people! These horrible people! These cold people! They never look at you." He shivered. "They never speak. They answer like dead men. They obey, these horrible people. And the girls are frozen!"

There was a light tap on the door and Joseph came in with a scuttle of coal. He moved silently through the room and set the scuttle down so softly that he made no noise, and he turned without looking up at anyone and went toward the door again. Prackle said loudly, "Joseph!" And Joseph turned without replying, without looking up, and he bowed very slightly. And Prackle said still loudly, "Joseph, is there any wine or any brandy?" Joseph shook his head.

Tonder started up from the table, his face wild with anger, and he shouted, "Answer, you swine! Answer in words!"

Joseph did not look up. He spoke tonelessly. "No, sir; no, sir, there is no wine."

And Tonder said furiously, "And no brandy?"

Joseph looked down and spoke tonelessly again. "There is no brandy, sir." He stood perfectly still.

"What do you want?" Tonder said.

"I want to go, sir."

"Then go, goddamn it!"

Joseph turned and went silently out of the room and Tonder took a handkerchief out of his pocket and wiped his face. Hunter looked up at him and said, "You shouldn't let him beat you so easily."

Tonder sat down in his chair and put his hands to his temples and he said brokenly, "I want a girl. I want to go home. I want a girl. There's a girl in this town, a pretty girl. I see her all the time. She has blond hair. She lives beside the old-iron store. I want that girl."

Prackle said, "Watch yourself. Watch your nerves."

At that moment the lights went out again and the room was in darkness. Hunter spoke while the matches were being struck and an attempt was being made to light the lanterns; he said, "I thought I had all of them. I must have missed one. But I can't be running down there all the time. I've got good men down there."

Tonder lighted the first lantern and then he lighted the other, and Hunter spoke sternly to Tonder. "Lieutenant, do your talking to us if you have to talk. Don't let the enemy hear you talk this way. There's nothing these people would like better than to know your nerves are getting thin. Don't let the enemy hear you."

Tonder sat down again. The light was sharp on his face and the hissing filled the room. He said, "That's it! The enemy's everywhere! Every man, every woman, even children! The enemy's everywhere! Their faces look out of doorways. The white faces behind the curtains, listening. We have beaten them, we have won everywhere, and they wait and obey, and they wait. Half the world is ours. Is it the same in other places, Major?"

And Hunter said, "I don't know."

"That's it," Tonder said. "We don't know. The reports—everything in hand. Conquered countries cheer our soldiers, cheer the new order." His voice changed and grew soft and still softer. "What do the reports say about us? Do they say we are cheered, loved, flowers in our paths? Oh, these horrible people waiting in the snow!"

And Hunter said, "Now that's off your chest, do you feel better?"

Prackle had been beating the table softly with his good fist, and he said, "He shouldn't talk that way. He should keep things to himself. He's a soldier, isn't he? Then let him be a soldier."

The door opened quietly and Captain Loft came in and there was snow on his helmet and snow on his shoulders. His nose was pinched and red and his overcoat collar was high about his ears. He took off his helmet and the snow fell to the floor and he brushed his shoulders. "What a job!" he said.

"More trouble?" Hunter asked.

"Always trouble. I see they've got your dynamo again. Well, I think I fixed the mine for a while."

"What's your trouble?" Hunter asked.

"Oh, the usual thing with me—the slow-down and a wrecked dump car. I saw the wrecker, though. I shot him. I think I have a cure for it, Major, now. I just thought it up. I'll make each man take out a certain amount of coal. I can't starve the men or they can't work, but I've really got the answer. If the coal doesn't come out, no food for the families. We'll have the men eat at the mine, so there's no dividing at home. That ought to cure it. They work or their kids don't eat. I told them just now."

"What did they say?"

Loft's eyes narrowed fiercely. "Say? What do they ever say? Nothing! Nothing at all! But we'll see whether the coal comes out now." He took off his coat and shook it, and his eyes fell on the entrance door and he saw that it was open a crack. He moved silently to the door, jerked it open, then closed it. "I thought I had closed that door tight," he said.

"You did," said Hunter.

Prackle still turned the pages of his illustrated paper. His voice was normal again. "Those are monster guns we're using in the east. I never saw one of them. Did you, Captain?"

"Oh, yes," said Captain Loft. "I've seen them fired. They're wonderful. Nothing can stand up against them."

Tonder said, "Captain, do you get much news from home?"

"A certain amount," said Loft.

"Is everything well there?"

"Wonderful!" said Loft. "The armies move ahead everywhere."

"The British aren't defeated yet?"

"They are defeated in every engagement."

"But they fight on?"

"A few air raids, no more."

"And the Russians?"

"It's all over."

Tonder said insistently, "But they fight on?"

"A little skirmishing, no more."

"Then we have just about won, haven't we, Captain?" Tonder asked.

"Yes, we have."

Tonder looked closely at him and said, "You believe this, don't you, Captain?"

Prackle broke in, "Don't let him start that again!"

Loft scowled at Tonder. "I don't know what you mean."

Tonder said, "I mean this: we'll be going home before long, won't we?"

"Well, the reorganization will take some time," Hunter said. "The new order can't be put into effect in a day, can it?"

Tonder said, "All our lives, perhaps?"

And Prackle said, "Don't let him start it again!"

Loft came very close to Tonder and he said, "Lieutenant, I don't like the tone of your questions. I don't like the tone of doubt."

Hunter looked up and said, "Don't be hard on him, Loft. He's tired. We're all tired."

"Well, I'm tired, too," said Loft, "but I don't let treasonable doubts get in."

Hunter said, "Don't bedevil him, I tell you! Where's the colonel, do you know?"

"He's making out his report. He's asking for reinforcements," said Loft. "It's a bigger job than we thought."

Prackle asked excitedly, "Will he get them—the reinforcements?"

"How would I know?"

Tonder smiled. "Reinforcements!" he said softly. "Or maybe replacements. Maybe we could go home for a while." And he said, smiling, "Maybe I could walk down the street and people would say, 'Hello,' and they'd say, 'There goes a soldier,' and they'd be glad for me and they'd be glad of me. And there'd be friends about, and I could turn my back to a man without being afraid."

Prackle said, "Don't start that again! Don't let him get out of hand again!"

And Loft said disgustedly, "We have enough trouble now without having the staff go crazy."

But Tonder went on, "You really think replacements will come, Captain?"

"I didn't say so."

"But you said they might."

"I said I didn't know. Look, Lieutenant, we've conquered half the world. We must police it for a while. You know that."

"But the other half?" Tonder asked.

"They will fight on hopelessly for a while," said Loft.

"Then we must be spread out all over."

"For a while," said Loft.

Prackle said nervously, "I wish you'd make him shut up. I wish you would shut him up. Make him stop it."

Tonder got out his handkerchief and blew his nose, and he spoke a little like a man out of his head. He laughed embarrassedly. He said, "I had a funny dream. I guess it was a dream. Maybe it was a thought. Maybe a thought or a dream."

Prackle said, "Make him stop, Captain!"

Tonder said, "Captain, is this place conquered?"

"Of course," said Loft.

A little note of hysteria crept into Tonder's laughter. He said, "Conquered and we're afraid; conquered and we're surrounded." His laughter grew shrill. "I had a dream—or a thought—out in the snow with the black shadows and the faces in the doorways, the cold faces behind curtains. I had a thought or a dream."

Prackle said, "Make him stop!"

Tonder said, "I dreamed the Leader was crazy."

And Loft and Hunter laughed together and Loft said, "The enemy have found out how crazy. I'll have to write that one home. The papers would print that

[118]

one. The enemy have learned how crazy the Leader is."

And Tonder went on laughing. "Conquest after conquest, deeper and deeper into molasses." His laughter choked him and he coughed into his handkerchief. "Maybe the Leader is crazy. Flies conquer the fly-paper. Flies capture two hundred miles of new fly-paper!" His laughter was growing more hysterical now.

Prackle leaned over and shook him with his good hand, "Stop it! You stop it! You have no right!"

And gradually Loft recognized that the laughter was hysterical and he stepped close to Tonder and slapped him in the face. He said, "Lieutenant, stop it!"

Tonder's laughter went on and Loft slapped him again in the face and he said, "Stop it, Lieutenant! Do you hear me?"

Suddenly Tonder's laughter stopped and the room was quiet except for the hissing of the lanterns. Tonder looked in amazement at his hand and he felt his bruised face with his hand and he looked at his hand again and his head sank down toward the table. "I want to go home," he said.

CHAPTER SIX

THERE was a little street not far from the town square where small peaked roofs and little shops were mixed up together. The snow was beaten down on the walks and in the street, but it piled high on the fences and it puffed on the roof peaks. It drifted against the shuttered windows of the little houses. And into the yards paths were shoveled. The night was dark and cold and no light showed from the windows to attract the bombers. And no one walked in the streets, for the curfew was strict. The houses were dark lumps against the snow. Every little while the patrol of six men walked down the street, peering about, and each man carried a long flashlight. The hushed tramp of their feet sounded in the street, the squeaks of their boots on the packed snow. They were muffled figures deep in thick coats; under their helmets were knitted caps which came down over their ears and covered their chins and mouths. A little snow fell, only a little, like rice.

The patrol talked as they walked, and they talked of things that they longed for—of meat and of hot soup and of the richness of butter, of the prettiness of girls and of their smiles and of their lips and their eyes. They talked of these things and sometimes they talked of their hatred of what they were doing and of their loneliness.

A small, peak-roofed house beside the iron shop was shaped like the others and wore its snow cap like the others. No light came from its shuttered windows and its storm doors were tightly closed. But inside a lamp burned in the small living-room and the door to the bedroom was open and the door to the kitchen was open. An iron stove was against the back wall with a little coal fire burning in it. It was a warm, poor, comfortable room, the floor covered with worn carpet, the walls papered in warm brown with an old-fashioned fleur-de-lis figure in gold. And on the back wall were two pictures, one of fish lying dead on a plate of ferns and the other of grouse lying dead on a fir bough. On the right wall there was a picture of Christ walking on the waves toward the despairing fishermen. Two straight chairs were in the room and a couch covered with a bright blanket. There was a little round table in the middle of the room, on which stood a kerosene lamp with a round flowered shade on it, and the light in the room was warm and soft.

The inner door, which led to the passage, which in turn led to the storm door, was beside the stove.

In a cushioned old rocking-chair beside the table Molly Morden sat alone. She was unraveling the wool from an old blue sweater and winding the yarn on a ball. She had quite a large ball of it. And on the table beside her was her knitting with the needles sticking in it, and a large pair of scissors. Her glasses lay on the table beside her, for she did not need them for knitting. She was pretty and young and neat. Her golden hair was done up on the top of her head and a blue bow was in her hair. Her hands worked quickly with the raveling. As she worked, she glanced now

[122]

and then at the door to the passage. The wind whistled in the chimney softly, but it was a quiet night, muffled with snow.

Suddenly she stopped her work. Her hands were still. She looked toward the door and listened. The tramping feet of the patrol went by in the street and the sound of their voices could be heard faintly. The sound faded away. Molly ripped out new yarn and wound it on the ball. And again she stopped. There was a rustle at the door and then three short knocks. Molly put down her work and went to the door.

"Yes?" she called.

She unlocked the door and opened it and a heavily cloaked figure came in. It was Annie, the cook, red-eyed and wrapped in mufflers. She slipped in quickly, as though practiced at getting speedily through doors and getting them closed again behind her. She stood there red-nosed, sniffling and glancing quickly around the room.

Molly said, "Good evening, Annie. I didn't expect you tonight. Take your things off and get warm. It's cold out."

Annie said, "The soldiers brought winter early. My father always said a war brought bad weather, or bad weather brought a war. I don't remember which."

"Take off your things and come to the stove."

"I can't," said Annie importantly. "They're coming."

"Who are coming?" Molly said.

"His Excellency," said Annie, "and the doctor and the two Anders boys."

"Here?" Molly asked. "What for?"

Annie held out her hand and there was a little package in it. "Take it," she said. "I stole it from the colonel's plate. It's meat."

And Molly unwrapped the little cake of meat and put it in her mouth and she spoke around her chewing. "Did you get some?"

Annie said, "I cook it, don't I? I always get some."

"When are they coming?"

Annie sniffled. "The Anders boys are sailing for England. They've got to. They're hiding now."

"Are they?" Molly asked. "What for?"

"Well, it was their brother, Jack, was shot today for wrecking that little car. The soldiers are looking for the rest of the family. You know how they do."

"Yes," Molly said, "I know how they do. Sit down, Annie."

"No time," said Annie. "I've got to get back and tell His Excellency it's all right here."

Molly said, "Did anybody see you come?"

Annie smiled proudly. "No, I'm awful good at sneaking."

"How will the Mayor get out?"

Annie laughed. "Joseph is going to be in his bed in case they look in, right in his nightshirt, right next to Madame!" And she laughed again. She said, "Joseph better lie pretty quiet."

Molly said, "It's an awful night to be sailing."

"It's better than being shot."

"Yes, so it is. Why is the Mayor coming here?"

"I don't know. He wants to talk to the Anders boys. I've got to go now, but I came to tell you."

Molly said, "How soon are they coming?"

"Oh, maybe half, maybe three-quarters of an hour," Annie said. "I'll come in first. Nobody bothers with old cooks." She started for the door and she turned midway, and as though accusing Molly of saying the last words she said truculently, "I'm not so old!" And she slipped out of the door and closed it behind her.

Molly went on knitting for a moment and then she got up and went to the stove and lifted the lid. The glow of the fire lighted her face. She stirred the fire and added a few lumps of coal and closed the stove again. Before she could get to her chair, there was a knocking on the outer door. She crossed the room and said to herself, "I wonder what she forgot." She went into the passage and she said, "What do you want?"

A man's voice answered her. She opened the door and a man's voice said, "I don't mean any harm. I don't mean any harm."

Molly backed into the room and Lieutenant Tonder followed her in. Molly said, "Who are you? What do you want? You can't come in here. What do you want?"

Lieutenant Tonder was dressed in his great gray overcoat. He entered the room and took off his helmet and he spoke pleadingly. "I don't mean any harm. Please let me come in."

Molly said, "What do you want?"

She shut the door behind him and he said, "Miss, I

only want to talk, that's all. I want to hear you talk. That's all I want."

"Are you forcing yourself on me?" Molly asked.

"No, miss, just let me stay a little while and then I'll go."

"What is it you want?"

Tonder tried to explain. "Can you understand this— can you believe this? Just for a little while, can't we forget this war? Just for a little while. Just for a little while, can't we talk together like people—together?"

Molly looked at him for a long time and then a smile came to her lips. "You don't know who I am, do you?"

Tonder said, "I've seen you in the town. I know you're lovely. I know I want to talk to you."

And Molly still smiled. She said softly, "You don't know who I am." She sat in her chair and Tonder stood like a child, looking very clumsy. Molly continued, speaking quietly, "Why, you're lonely. It's as simple as that, isn't it?"

Tonder licked his lips and he spoke eagerly. "That's it," he said. "You understand. I knew you would. I knew you'd have to." His words came tumbling out.

"I'm lonely to the point of illness. I'm lonely in the quiet and the hatred." And he said pleadingly, "Can't we talk, just a little bit?"

Molly picked up her knitting. She looked quickly at the front door. "You can stay not more than fifteen minutes. Sit down a little, Lieutenant."

She looked at the door again. The house creaked. Tonder became tense and he said, "Is someone here?"

"No, the snow is heavy on the roof. I have no man any more to push it down."

Tonder said gently, "Who did it? Was it something we did?"

And Molly nodded, looking far off. "Yes."

He sat down. "I'm sorry." After a moment he said, "I wish I could do something. I'll have the snow pushed off the roof."

"No," said Molly, "no."

"Why not?"

"Because the people would think I had joined with you. They would expel me. I don't want to be expelled."

Tonder said, "Yes, I see how that would be. You all hate us. But I'll take care of you if you'll let me."

Now Molly knew she was in control, and her eyes narrowed a little cruelly and she said, "Why do you ask? You are the conqueror. Your men don't have to ask. They take what they want."

"That's not what I want," Tonder said. "That's not the way I want it."

And Molly laughed, still a little cruelly. "You want me to like you, don't you, Lieutenant?"

He said simply, "Yes," and he raised his head and he said, "You are so beautiful, so warm. Your hair is bright. Oh, I've seen no kindness in a woman's face for so long!"

"Do you see any in mine?" she asked.

He looked closely at her. "I want to."

She dropped her eyes at last. "You're making love to me, aren't you, Lieutenant?"

And he said clumsily, "I want you to like me. Surely I want you to like me. Surely I want to see that in your eyes. I have seen you in the streets. I have watched you pass by. I've given orders that you mustn't be molested. Have you been molested?"

And Molly said quietly, "Thank you; no, I've not been molested."

His words rushed on. "Why, I've even written a poem for you. Would you like to see my poem?"

And she said sardonically, "Is it a long poem? You have to go very soon."

He said, "No, it's a little tiny poem. It's a little bit of a poem." He reached inside his tunic and brought out a folded paper and handed it to her. She leaned close to the lamp and put on her glasses and she read quietly.

> *Your eyes in their deep heavens*
> *Possess me and will not depart;*
> *A sea of blue thoughts rushing*
> *And pouring over my heart.*

She folded the paper and put it in her lap. "Did you write this, Lieutenant?"

"Yes."

She said a little tauntingly, "To me?"

And Tonder answered uneasily, "Yes."

She looked at him steadily, smiling. "You didn't write it, Lieutenant, did you?"

He smiled back like a child caught in a lie. "No."

Molly asked him, "Do you know who did?"

Tonder said, "Yes, Heine wrote it. It's *'Mit deinen*

blauen Augen.' I've always loved it." He laughed embarrassedly and Molly laughed with him, and suddenly they were laughing together. He stopped laughing just as suddenly and a bleakness came into his eyes. "I haven't laughed like that since forever." He said, "They told us the people would like us, would admire us. They do not. They only hate us." And then he changed the subject as though he worked against time. "You are so beautiful. You are as beautiful as the laughter."

Molly said, "You're beginning to make love to me, Lieutenant. You must go in a moment."

And Tonder said, "Maybe I want to make love to you. A man needs love. A man dies without love. His insides shrivel and his chest feels like a dry chip. I'm lonely."

Molly got up from her chair. She looked nervously at the door and she walked to the stove and, coming back, her face grew hard and her eyes grew punishing and she said, "Do you want to go to bed with me, Lieutenant?"

"I didn't say that! Why do you talk that way?"

Molly said cruelly, "Maybe I'm trying to disgust

you. I was married once. My husband is dead. You see, I'm not a virgin." Her voice was bitter.

Tonder said, "I only want you to like me."

And Molly said, "I know. You are a civilized man. You know that love-making is more full and whole and delightful if there is liking, too."

Tonder said, "Don't talk that way! Please don't talk that way!"

Molly glanced quickly at the door. She said, "We are a conquered people, Lieutenant. You have taken the food away. I'm hungry. I'll like you better if you feed me."

Tonder said, "What are you saying?"

"Do I disgust you, Lieutenant? Maybe I'm trying to. My price is two sausages."

Tonder said, "You can't talk this way!"

"What about your own girls, Lieutenant, after the last war? A man could choose among your girls for an egg or a slice of bread. Do you want me for nothing, Lieutenant? Is the price too high?"

He said, "You fooled me for a moment. But you hate me, too, don't you? I thought maybe you wouldn't."

"No, I don't hate you," she said, "I'm hungry and—I hate you!"

Tonder said, "I'll give you anything you need, but——"

And she interrupted him. "You want to call it something else? You don't want a whore. Is that what you mean?"

Tonder said, "I don't know what I mean. You make it sound full of hatred."

Molly laughed. She said, "It's not nice to be hungry. Two sausages, two fine, fat sausages can be the most precious things in the world."

"Don't say those things," he said. "Please don't!"

"Why not? They're true."

"They aren't true! This can't be true!"

She looked at him for a moment and then she sat down and her eyes fell to her lap and she said, "No, it's not true. I don't hate you. I'm lonely, too. And the snow is heavy on the roof."

Tonder got up and moved near to her. He took one of her hands in both of his and he said softly, "Please don't hate me. I'm only a lieutenant. I didn't ask to come here. You didn't ask to be my enemy. I'm only a man, not a conquering man."

Molly's fingers encircled his hand for a moment and she said softly, "I know; yes, I know."

And Tonder said, "We have some little right to life in all this death."

She put her hand to his cheek for a moment and she said, "Yes."

"I'll take care of you," he said. "We have some right to life in all the killing." His hand rested on her shoulder. Suddenly she grew rigid and her eyes were wide and staring as though she saw a vision. His hand released her and he asked, "What's the matter? What is it?" Her eyes stared straight ahead and he repeated, "What is it?"

Molly spoke in a haunted voice. "I dressed him like a little boy for his first day in school. And he was afraid. I buttoned his shirt and tried to comfort him, but he was beyond comfort. And he was afraid."

Tonder said, "What are you saying?"

And Molly seemed to see what she described. "I don't know why they let him come home. He was confused. He didn't know what was happening. He didn't even kiss me when he went away. He was afraid, and very brave, like a little boy on his first day of school."

Tonder stood up. "That was your husband."

Molly said, "Yes, my husband. I went to the Mayor, but he was helpless. And then he marched away—not very well nor steadily—and you took him out and you shot him. It was more strange than terrible then. I didn't quite believe it then."

Tonder said, "Your husband!"

"Yes; and now in the quiet house, I believe it. Now with the heavy snow on the roof, I believe it. And in the loneliness before daybreak, in the half-warmed bed, I know it then."

Tonder stood in front of her. His face was full of misery. "Good night," he said. "God keep you. May I come back?"

And Molly looked at the wall and at the memory. "I don't know," she said.

"I'll come back."

"I don't know."

He looked at her and then he quietly went out of the door, and Molly still stared at the wall. "God keep me!" She stayed for a moment staring at the wall. The door opened silently and Annie came in. Molly did not even see her.

Annie said disapprovingly, "The door was open."

Molly looked slowly toward her, her eyes still wide open. "Yes. Oh, yes, Annie."

"The door was open. There was a man came out. I saw him. He looked like a soldier."

And Molly said, "Yes, Annie."

"Was it a soldier here?"

"Yes, it was a soldier."

And Annie asked suspiciously, "What was he doing here?"

"He came to make love to me."

Annie said, "Miss, what are you doing? You haven't joined them, have you? You aren't with them, like that Corell?"

"No, I'm not with them, Annie."

Annie said, "If the Mayor's here and they come back, it'll be your fault if anything happens; it'll be your fault!"

"He won't come back. I won't let him come back."

But the suspicion stayed with Annie. She said, "Shall I tell them to come in now? Do you say it's safe?"

"Yes, it's safe. Where are they?"

"They're out behind the fence," said Annie.

"Tell them to come in."

And while Annie went out, Molly got up and smoothed her hair and she shook her head, trying to be alive again. There was a little sound in the passage. Two tall, blond young men entered. They were dressed in pea-jackets and dark turtle-neck sweaters. They wore stocking caps perched on their heads. They were wind-burned and strong and they looked almost like twins, Will Anders and Tom Anders, the fishermen.

"Good evening, Molly. You've heard?"

"Annie told me. It's a bad night to go."

Tom said, "It's better than a clear night. The planes see you on a clear night. What's the Mayor want, Molly?"

"I don't know. I heard about your brother. I'm sorry."

The two were silent and they looked embarrassed. Tom said, "You know how it is, better than most."

"Yes; yes, I know."

Annie came in the door again and she said in a hoarse whisper, "They're here!" And Mayor Orden and Doctor Winter came in. They took off their coats and caps and laid them on the couch. Orden went to Molly and kissed her on the forehead.

"Good evening, dear."

He turned to Annie. "Stand in the passage, Annie. Give us one knock for the patrol, one when it's gone, and two for danger. You can leave the outer door open a crack so you can hear if anyone comes."

Annie said, "Yes, sir." She went into the passage and shut the door behind her.

Doctor Winter was at the stove, warming his hands. "We got word you boys were going tonight."

"We've got to go," Tom said.

Orden nodded. "Yes, I know. We heard you were going to take Mr. Corell with you."

Tom laughed bitterly. "We thought it would be only right. We're taking his boat. We can't leave him around. It isn't good to see him in the streets."

Orden said sadly, "I wish he had gone away. It's just a danger to you, taking him."

"It isn't good to see him in the streets," Will echoed his brother. "It isn't good for the people to see him here."

Winter asked, "Can you take him? Isn't he cautious at all?"

"Oh, yes, he's cautious, in a way. At twelve o'clock, though, he walks to his house usually. We'll be behind the wall. I think we can get him through his lower garden to the water. His boat's tied up there. We were on her today getting her ready."

Orden repeated, "I wish you didn't have to. It's just an added danger. If he makes a noise, the patrol might come."

Tom said, "He won't make a noise, and it's better if he disappears at sea. Some of the town people might get him and then there would be too much killing. No, it's better if he goes to sea."

Molly took up her knitting again. She said, "Will you throw him overboard?"

Will blushed. "He'll go to sea, ma'am." He turned to the Mayor. "You wanted to see us, sir?"

"Why, yes, I want to talk to you. Doctor Winter and I have tried to think—there's so much talk about justice, injustice, conquest. Our people are invaded, but I don't think they're conquered."

There was a sharp knock on the door and the room

was silent. Molly's needles stopped, and the Mayor's outstretched hand remained in the air. Tom, scratching his ear, left his hand there and stopped scratching. Everyone in the room was motionless. Every eye was turned toward the door. Then, first faintly and then growing louder, there came the tramp of the patrol, the squeak of their boots in the snow, and the sound of their talking as they went by. They passed the door and their footsteps disappeared in the distance. There was a second tap on the door. And in the room the people relaxed.

Orden said, "It must be cold out there for Annie." He took up his coat from the couch and opened the inner door and handed his coat through. "Put this around your shoulders, Annie," he said and closed the door.

"I don't know what I'd do without her," he said, "She gets everywhere, she sees and hears everything."

Tom said, "We should be going pretty soon, sir."

And Winter said, "I wish you'd forget about Mr. Corell."

"We can't. It isn't good to see him in the streets." He looked inquiringly at Mayor Orden.

Orden began slowly. "I want to speak simply. This is a little town. Justice and injustice are in terms of little things. Your brother's shot and Alex Morden's shot. Revenge against a traitor. The people are angry and they have no way to fight back. But it's all in little terms. It's people against people, not idea against idea."

Winter said, "It's funny for a doctor to think of destruction, but I think all invaded people want to resist. We are disarmed; our spirits and bodies aren't enough. The spirit of a disarmed man sinks."

Will Anders asked, "What's all this for, sir? What do you want of us?"

"We want to fight them and we can't," Orden said. "They're using hunger on the people now. Hunger brings weakness. You boys are sailing for England. Maybe nobody will listen to you, but tell them from us—from a small town—to give us weapons."

Tom asked, "You want guns?"

Again there was a quick knock on the door and the people froze where they were, and from outside there came the sound of the patrol, but at double step, running. Will moved quickly toward the door. The running steps came abreast of the house. There were muffled orders and the patrol ran by, and there was a second tap at the door.

Molly said, "They must be after somebody. I wonder who this time."

"We should be going," Tom said uneasily. "Do you want guns, sir? Shall we ask for guns?"

"No, tell them how it is. We are watched. Any move we make calls for reprisal. If we could have simple, secret weapons, weapons of stealth, explosives, dynamite to blow up rails, grenades, if possible, even poison." He spoke angrily. "This is no honorable war. This is a war of treachery and murder. Let us use the methods that have been used on us! Let the British bombers drop their big bombs on the works, but let them also drop us little bombs to use, to hide, to slip under the rails, under tanks. Then we will be armed, secretly armed. Then the invader will never know which of us is armed. Let the bombers bring us simple weapons. We will know how to use them!"

Winter broke in. "They'll never know where it will strike. The soldiers, the patrol, will never know which of us is armed."

Tom wiped his forehead. "If we get through, we'll tell them, sir, but—well, I've heard it said that in England there are still men in power who do not dare to put weapons in the hands of common people."

Orden stared at him. "Oh! I hadn't thought of that. Well, we can only see. If such people still govern England and America, the world is lost, anyway. Tell them what we say, if they will listen. We must have help, but if we get it"—his face grew very hard—"if we get it, we will help ourselves."

Winter said, "If they will even give us dynamite to hide, to bury in the ground to be ready against need, then the invader can never rest again, never! We will blow up his supplies."

The room grew excited. Molly said fiercely, "Yes, we could fight his rest, then. We could fight his sleep. We could fight his nerves and his certainties."

Will asked quietly, "Is that all, sir?"

"Yes." Orden nodded. "That's the core of it."

"What if they won't listen?"

"You can only try, as you are trying the sea tonight."

"Is that all, sir?"

The door opened and Annie came quietly in. Orden went on, "That's all. If you have to go now, let me send Annie out to see that the way is clear." He looked up and saw that Annie had come in. Annie said, "There's a soldier coming up the path. He looks like the soldier that was here before. There was a soldier here with Molly before."

The others looked at Molly. Annie said, "I locked the door."

"What does he want?" Molly asked. "Why does he come back?"

There was a gentle knocking at the outside door. Orden went to Molly. "What is this, Molly? Are you in trouble?"

"No," she said, "no! Go out the back way. You can get out through the back. Hurry, hurry out!"

The knocking continued on the front door. A man's voice called softly. Molly opened the door to the kitchen. She said, "Hurry, hurry!"

The Mayor stood in front of her. "Are you in trouble, Molly? You haven't done anything?"

Annie said coldly, "It looks like the same soldier. There was a soldier here before."

"Yes," Molly said to the Mayor. "Yes, there was a soldier here before."

The Mayor said, "What did he want?"

"He wanted to make love to me."

"But he didn't?" Orden said.

"No," she said, "he didn't. Go now, and I'll take care."

Orden said, "Molly, if you're in trouble, let us help you."

"The trouble I'm in no one can help me with," she said. "Go now," and she pushed them out of the door.

Annie remained behind. She looked at Molly. "Miss, what does this soldier want?"

"I don't know what he wants."

"Are you going to tell him anything?"

"No." Wonderingly, Molly repeated, "No." And then sharply she said, "No, Annie, I'm not!"

Annie scowled at her. "Miss, you'd better not tell him anything!" And she went out and closed the door behind her.

The tapping continued on the front door and a man's voice could be heard through the door.

Molly went to the center lamp, and her burden was

heavy on her. She looked down at the lamp. She looked at the table, and she saw the big scissors lying beside her knitting. She picked them up wonderingly by the blades. The blades slipped through her fingers until she held the long shears and she was holding them like a knife, and her eyes were horrified. She looked down into the lamp and the light flooded up in her face. Slowly she raised the shears and placed them inside her dress.

The tapping continued on the door. She heard the voice calling to her. She leaned over the lamp for a moment and then suddenly she blew out the light. The room was dark except for a spot of red that came from the coal stove. She opened the door. Her voice was strained and sweet. She called, "I'm coming, Lieutenant, I'm coming!"

CHAPTER SEVEN

In the dark, clear night a white, half-withered moon brought little light. The wind was dry and singing over the snow, a quiet wind that blew steadily, evenly from the cold point of the Pole. Over the land the snow lay very deep and dry as sand. The houses snuggled down in the hollows of banked snow, and their windows were dark and shuttered against the cold, and only a little smoke rose from the banked fires.

In the town the footpaths were frozen hard and packed hard. And the streets were silent, too, except when the miserable, cold patrol came by. The houses were dark against the night, and a little lingering warmth remained in the houses against the morning. Near the mine entrance the guards watched the sky and trained their instruments on the sky and turned their listening-instruments against the sky, for it was a clear night for bombing. On nights like this the feathered steel spindles came whistling down and roared to splinters. The land would be visible from the sky tonight, even though the moon seemed to throw little light.

Down toward one end of the village, among the small houses, a dog complained about the cold and the loneliness. He raised his nose to his god and gave a long and fulsome account of the state of the world as it applied to him. He was a practiced singer with a full bell throat and great versatility of range and control. The six men of the patrol slogging dejectedly up and down the streets heard the singing of the dog, and one of the muffled soldiers said, "Seems to me he's getting worse every night. I suppose we ought to shoot him."

And another answered, "Why? Let him howl. He sounds good to me. I used to have a dog at home that howled. I never could break him. Yellow dog. I don't mind the howl. They took my dog when they took the others," he said factually, in a dull voice.

And the corporal said, "Couldn't have dogs eating up food that was needed."

"Oh, I'm not complaining. I know it was necessary. I can't plan the way the leaders do. It seems funny to me, though, that some people here have dogs, and they don't have even as much food as we have. They're pretty gaunt, though, dogs and people."

"They're fools," said the corporal. "That's why they lost so quickly. They can't plan the way we can."

"I wonder if we'll have dogs again after it's over," said the soldier. "I suppose we could get them from America or some place and start the breeds again. What kind of dogs do you suppose they have in America?"

"I don't know," said the corporal. "Probably dogs as crazy as everything else they have." And he went on, "Maybe dogs are no good, anyway. It might be just as well if we never bothered with them, except for police work."

"It might be," said the soldier. "I've heard the Leader doesn't like dogs. I've heard they make him itch and sneeze."

"You hear all kinds of things," the corporal said.

"Listen!" The patrol stopped and from a great distance came the bee hum of planes.

"There they come," the corporal said. "Well, there aren't any lights. It's been two weeks, hasn't it, since they came before?"

"Twelve days," said the soldier.

The guards at the mine heard the high drone of the planes. "They're flying high," a sergeant said. And Captain Loft tilted his head back so that he could see under the rim of his helmet. "I judge over 20,000 feet," he said. "Maybe they're going on over."

"Aren't very many." The sergeant listened. "I don't think there are more than three of them. Shall I call the battery?"

"Just see they're alert, and then call Colonel Lanser—no, don't call him. Maybe they aren't coming here. They're nearly over and they haven't started to dive yet."

"Sounds to me like they're circling. I don't think there are more than two," the sergeant said.

In their beds the people heard the planes and they squirmed deep into their featherbeds and listened. In the palace of the Mayor the little sound awakened

Colonel Lanser, and he turned over on his back and looked at the dark ceiling with wide-open eyes, and he held his breath to listen better and then his heart beat so that he could not hear as well as he could when he was breathing. Mayor Orden heard the planes in his sleep and they made a dream for him and he moved and whispered in his sleep.

High in the air the two bombers circled, mud-colored planes. They cut their throttles and soared, circling. And from the belly of each one tiny little objects dropped, hundreds of them, one after another. They plummeted a few feet and then little parachutes opened and drifted small packages silently and slowly downward toward the earth, and the planes raised their throttles and gained altitude, and then cut their throttles and circled again, and more of the little objects plummeted down, and then the planes turned and flew back in the direction from which they had come.

The tiny parachutes floated like thistledown and the breeze spread them out and distributed them as seeds on the ends of thistledown are distributed. They drifted so slowly and landed so gently that sometimes the ten-inch packages of dynamite stood upright in the snow, and the little parachutes folded gently down around them. They looked black against the snow. They landed in the white fields and among the woods of the hills and they landed in trees and hung down from the branches. Some of them landed on the house-tops of the little town, some in the small front yards, and one landed and stood upright in the snow crown on top of the head of the village statue of St. Albert the Missionary.

One of the little parachutes came down in the street ahead of the patrol and the sergeant said, "Careful! It's a time bomb."

"It ain't big enough," a soldier said.

"Well, don't go near it." The sergeant had his flash-light out and he turned it on the object, a little para-chute no bigger than a handkerchief, colored light blue, and hanging from it a package wrapped in blue paper.

"Now don't anybody touch it," the sergeant said. "Harry, you go down to the mine and get the captain. We'll keep an eye on this damn thing."

The late dawn came and the people moving out of

their houses in the country saw the spots of blue against the snow. They went to them and picked them up. They unwrapped the paper and read the printed words. They saw the gift and suddenly each finder grew furtive, and he concealed the long tube under his coat and went to some secret place and hid the tube.

And word got to the children about the gift and they combed the countryside in a terrible Easter egg hunt, and when some lucky child saw the blue color, he rushed to the prize and opened it and then he hid the tube and told his parents about it. There were some people who were frightened, who turned the tubes over to the military, but they were not very many. And the soldiers scurried about the town in another Easter egg hunt, but they were not so good at it as the children were.

In the drawing-room of the palace of the Mayor the dining-table remained with the chairs about as it had been placed the day Alex Morden was shot. The room had not the grace it had when it was still the palace of the Mayor. The walls, bare of standing chairs, looked very blank. The table with a few papers scattered about on it made the room look like a business office.

The clock on the mantel struck nine. It was a dark day now, overcast with clouds, for the dawn had brought the heavy snow clouds.

Annie came out of the Mayor's room; she swooped by the table and glanced at the papers that lay there. Captain Loft came in. He stopped in the doorway, seeing Annie.

"What are you doing here?" he demanded.

And Annie said sullenly, "Yes, sir."

"I said, what are you doing here?"

"I thought to clean up, sir."

"Let things alone, and go along."

And Annie said, "Yes, sir," and she waited until he was clear of the door, and she scuttled out.

Captain Loft turned back through the doorway and he said, "All right, bring it in." A soldier came through the door behind him, his rifle hung over his shoulder by a strap, and in his arms he held a number of the blue packages, and from the ends of the packages there dangled the little strings and pieces of blue cloth.

Loft said, "Put them on the table." The soldier gingerly laid the packages down. "Now go upstairs and report to Colonel Lanser that I'm here with the—

things," and the soldier wheeled about and left the room.

Loft went to the table and picked up one of the packages, and his face wore a look of distaste. He held up the little blue cloth parachute, held it above his head and dropped it, and the cloth opened and the package floated to the floor. He picked up the package again and examined it.

Now Colonel Lanser came quickly into the room, followed by Major Hunter. Hunter was carrying a square of yellow paper in his hand. Lanser said, "Good morning, Captain," and he went to the head of the table and sat down. For a moment he looked at the little pile of tubes, and then he picked one up and held it in his hand. "Sit down, Hunter," he said. "Have you examined these?"

Hunter pulled out a chair and sat down. He looked at the yellow paper in his hand. "Not very carefully," he said. "There are three breaks in the railroad all within ten miles."

"Well, take a look at them and see what you think," Lanser said.

Hunter reached for a tube and stripped off the outer

covering, and inside was a small package next to the tube. Hunter took out a knife and cut into the tube. Captain Loft looked over his shoulder. Then Hunter smelled the cut and rubbed his fingers together, and he said, "It's silly. It's commercial dynamite. I don't know what per cent of nitroglycerin until I test it." He looked at the end. "It has a regular dynamite cap, fulminate of mercury, and a fuse—about a minute, I suppose." He tossed the tube back onto the table. "It's very cheap and very simple," he said.

The colonel looked at Loft. "How many do you think were dropped?"

"I don't know, sir," said Loft. "We picked up about fifty of them, and about ninety parachutes they came in. For some reason the people leave the parachutes when they take the tubes, and then there are probably a lot we haven't found yet."

Lanser waved his hand. "It doesn't really matter," he said. "They can drop as many as they want. We can't stop it, and we can't use it against them, either. They haven't conquered anybody."

Loft said fiercely, "We can beat them off the face of the earth!"

Hunter was prying the copper cap out of the top of one of the sticks, and Lanser said, "Yes—we can do that. Have you looked at this wrapper, Hunter?"

"Not yet, I haven't had time."

"It's kind of devilish, this thing," said Colonel Lanser. "The wrapper is blue, so that it's easy to see. Unwrap the outer paper and here"—he picked up the small package—"here is a piece of chocolate. Everybody will be looking for it. I'll bet our own soldiers steal the chocolate. Why, the kids will be looking for them, like Easter eggs."

A soldier came in and laid a square of yellow paper in front of the colonel and retired, and Lanser glanced at it and laughed harshly. "Here's something for you, Hunter. Two more breaks in your line."

Hunter looked up from the copper cap he was examining, and he asked, "How general is this? Did they drop them everywhere?"

Lanser was puzzled. "Now, that's the funny thing. I've talked to the capital. This is the only place they've dropped them."

"What do you make of that?" Hunter asked.

"Well, it's hard to say. I think this is a test place. I

suppose if it works here they'll use it all over, and if it doesn't work here they won't bother."

"What are you going to do?" Hunter asked.

"The capital orders me to stamp this out so ruthlessly that they won't drop it any place else."

Hunter said plaintively, "How am I going to mend five breaks in the railroad? I haven't rails right now for five breaks."

"You'll have to rip out some of the old sidings, I guess," said Lanser.

Hunter said, "That'll make a hell of a roadbed."

"Well, anyway, it will make a roadbed."

Major Hunter tossed the tube he had torn apart onto the pile, and Loft broke in, "We must stop this thing at once, sir. We must arrest and punish people who pick these things up, before they use them. We have to get busy so these people won't think we are weak."

Lanser was smiling at him, and he said, "Take it easy, Captain. Let's see what we have first, and then we'll think of remedies."

He took a new package from the pile and unwrapped it. He took the little piece of chocolate, tasted it, and he said, "This is a devilish thing. It's good chocolate, too. I can't even resist it myself. The prize in the grab-bag." Then he picked up the dynamite. "What do you think of this really, Hunter?"

"What I told you. It's very cheap and very effective for small jobs, dynamite with a cap and a one-minute fuse. It's good if you know how to use it. It's no good if you don't."

Lanser studied the print on the inside of the wrapper. "Have you read this?"

"Glanced at it," said Hunter.

"Well, I have read it, and I want you to listen to it carefully," said Lanser. He read from the paper, "'To the unconquered people: Hide this. Do not expose yourself. You will need this later. It is a present from your friends to you and from you to the invader of your country. Do not try to do large things with it.'" He began to skip through the bill. "Now here, 'rails in the country.' And, 'work at night.' And, 'tie up transportation.' Now here, 'Instructions: rails. Place stick under rail close to the joint, and tight against a tie. Pack mud or hard-beaten snow around it so that it is firm. When the fuse is lighted you have a slow count of sixty before it explodes.'"

He looked up at Hunter and Hunter said simply, "It works." Lanser looked back at his paper and he skipped through. " 'Bridges: Weaken, do not destroy.' And here, 'transmission poles,' and here, 'culverts, trucks.' " He laid the blue handbill down. "Well, there it is."

Loft said angrily, "We must do something! There must be a way to control this. What does headquarters say?"

Lanser pursed his lips and his fingers played with one of the tubes. "I could have told you what they'd say before they said it. I have the orders. 'Set booby traps and poison the chocolate.' " He paused for a moment and then he said, "Hunter, I'm a good, loyal man, but sometimes when I hear the brilliant ideas of headquarters, I wish I were a civilian, an old, crippled civilian. They always think they are dealing with stupid people. I don't say that this is a measure of their intelligence, do I?"

Hunter looked amused. "Do you?"

Lanser said sharply, "No, I don't. But what will happen? One man will pick up one of these and get blown to bits by our booby trap. One kid will eat chocolate and die of strychnine poisoning. And then?" He looked down at his hands. "They will poke them with poles, or lasso them, before they touch them. They will try the chocolate on the cat. Goddamn it, Major, these are intelligent people. Stupid traps won't catch them twice."

Loft cleared his throat. "Sir, this is defeatist talk," he said. "We must do something. Why do you suppose it was only dropped here, sir?"

And Lanser said, "For one of two reasons: either this town was picked at random or else there is communication between this town and the outside. We know that some of the young men have got away."

Loft repeated dully, "We must do something, sir."

Now Lanser turned on him. "Loft, I think I'll recommend you for the General Staff. You want to get to work before you even know what the problem is. This is a new kind of conquest. Always before, it was possible to disarm a people and keep them in ignorance. Now they listen to their radios and we can't stop them. We can't even find their radios."

A soldier looked in through the doorway. "Mr. Corell to see you, sir."

Lanser replied, "Tell him to wait." He continued to talk to Loft. "They read the handbills; weapons drop from the sky for them. Now it's dynamite, Captain. Pretty soon it may be grenades, and then poison."

Loft said anxiously, "They haven't dropped poison yet."

"No, but they will. Can you think what will happen to the morale of our men or even to you if the people had some of those little game darts, you know, those silly little things you throw at a target, the points coated perhaps with cyanide, silent, deadly little things that you couldn't hear coming, that would pierce the uniform and make no noise? And what if our men knew that arsenic was about? Would you or they drink or eat comfortably?"

Hunter said dryly, "Are you writing the enemy's campaign, Colonel?"

"No, I'm trying to anticipate it."

Loft said, "Sir, we sit here talking when we should be searching for this dynamite. If there is organization among these people, we have to find it, we have to stamp it out."

"Yes," said Lanser, "we have to stamp it out, ferociously, I suppose. You take a detail, Loft. Get Prackle to take one. I wish we had more junior officers. Tonder's getting killed didn't help us a bit. Why couldn't he let women alone?"

Loft said, "I don't like the way Lieutenant Prackle is acting, sir."

"What's he doing?"

"He isn't doing anything, but he's jumpy and he's gloomy."

"Yes," Lanser said, "I know. It's a thing I've talked about so much. You know," he said, "I might be a major-general if I hadn't talked about it so much. We trained our young men for victory and you've got to admit they're glorious in victory, but they don't quite know how to act in defeat. We told them they were brighter and braver than other young men. It was a kind of shock to them to find out that they aren't a bit braver or brighter than other young men."

Loft said harshly, "What do you mean by defeat? We are not defeated."

And Lanser looked coldly up at him for a long moment and did not speak, and finally Loft's eyes wavered, and he said, "Sir."

"Thank you," said Lanser.

"You don't demand it of the others, sir."

"They don't think about it, so it isn't an insult. When you leave it out, it's insulting."

"Yes, sir," said Loft.

"Go on, now, try to keep Prackle in hand. Start your search. I don't want any shooting unless there's an overt act, do you understand?"

"Yes, sir," said Loft, and he saluted formally and went out of the room.

Hunter regarded Colonel Lanser amusedly. "Weren't you rough on him?"

"I had to be. He's frightened. I know his kind. He has to be disciplined when he's afraid or he'll go to pieces. He relies on discipline the way other men rely on sympathy. I suppose you'd better get to your rails. You might as well expect that tonight is the time when they'll really blow them, though."

Hunter stood up and he said, "Yes. I suppose the orders are coming in from the capital?"

"Yes."

"Are they——"

"You know what they are," Lanser interrupted. "You

know what they'd have to be. Take the leaders, shoot the leaders, take hostages, shoot the hostages, take more hostages, shoot them"—his voice had risen but now it sank almost to a whisper—"and the hatred growing and the hurt between us deeper and deeper."

Hunter hesitated. "Have they condemned any from the list of names?" and he motioned slightly toward the Mayor's bedroom.

Lanser shook his head. "No, not yet. They are just arrested so far."

Hunter said quietly, "Colonel, do you want me to recommend—maybe you're overtired, Colonel? Could I—you know—could I report that you're overtired?"

For a moment Lanser covered his eyes with his hand, and then his shoulders straightened and his face grew hard. "I'm not a civilian, Hunter. We're short enough of officers already. You know that. Get to your work, Major. I have to see Corell."

Hunter smiled. He went to the door and opened it, and he said out of the door, "Yes, he's here," and over his shoulder he said to Lanser, "It's Prackle. He wants to see you."

"Send him in," said Lanser.

Prackle came in, his face sullen, belligerent. "Colonel Lanser, sir, I wish to——"

"Sit down," said Lanser. "Sit down and rest a moment. Be a good soldier, Lieutenant."

The stiffness went out of Prackle quickly. He sat down beside the table and rested his elbows on it. "I wish——"

And Lanser said, "Don't talk for a moment. I know what it is. You didn't think it would be this way, did you? You thought it would be rather nice."

"They hate us," Prackle said. "They hate us so much."

Lanser smiled. "I wonder if I know what it is. It takes young men to make good soldiers, and young men need young women, is that it?"

"Yes, that's it."

"Well," Lanser said kindly, "does she hate you?"

Prackle looked at him in amazement. "I don't know, sir. Sometimes I think she's only sorry."

"And you're pretty miserable?"

"I don't like it here, sir."

"No, you thought it would be fun, didn't you? Lieutenant Tonder went to pieces and then he went out and they got a knife in him. I could send you home.

Do you want to be sent home, knowing we need you here?"

Prackle said uneasily, "No, sir, I don't."

"Good. Now I'll tell you, and I hope you'll understand it. You're not a man any more. You are a soldier. Your comfort is of no importance and, Lieutenant, your life isn't of much importance. If you live, you will have memories. That's about all you will have. Meanwhile you must take orders and carry them out. Most of the orders will be unpleasant, but that's not your business. I will not lie to you, Lieutenant. They should have trained you for this, and not for flower-strewn streets. They should have built your soul with truth, not led it along with lies." His voice grew hard. "But you took the job, Lieutenant. Will you stay with it or quit it? We can't take care of your soul."

Prackle stood up. "Thank you, sir."

"And the girl," Lanser continued, "the girl, Lieutenant, you may rape her, or protect her, or marry her—that is of no importance so long as you shoot her when it is ordered."

Prackle said wearily, "Yes, sir, thank you, sir."

"I assure you it is better to know. I assure you of

that. It is better to know. Go now, Lieutenant, and if Corell is still waiting, send him in." And he watched Lieutenant Prackle out of the doorway.

When Mr. Corell came in, he was a changed man. His left arm was in a cast, and he was no longer the jovial, friendly, smiling Corell. His face was sharp and bitter, and his eyes squinted down like little dead pig's eyes.

"I should have come before, Colonel," he said, "but your lack of co-operation made me hesitant."

Lanser said, "You were waiting for a reply to your report, I remember."

"I was waiting for much more than that. You refused me a position of authority. You said I was valueless. You did not realize that I was in this town long before you were. You left the Mayor in his office, contrary to my advice."

Lanser said, "Without him here we might have had more disorder than we have."

"That is a matter of opinion," Corell said. "This man is a leader of a rebellious people."

"Nonsense," said Lanser; "he's just a simple man."

With his good hand Corell took a black notebook

from his right pocket and opened it with his fingers. "You forgot, Colonel, that I had my sources, that I had been here a long time before you. I have to report to you that Mayor Orden has been in constant contact with every happening in this community. On the night when Lieutenant Tonder was murdered, he was in the house where the murder was committed. When the girl escaped to the hills, she stayed with one of his relatives. I traced her there, but she was gone. Whenever men have escaped, Orden has known about it and has helped them. And I even strongly suspect that he is somewhere in the picture of these little parachutes."

Lanser said eagerly, "But you can't prove it."

"No," Corell said, "I can't prove it. The first thing I know; the last I only suspect. Perhaps now you will be willing to listen to me."

Lanser said quietly, "What do you suggest?"

"These suggestions, Colonel, are a little stronger than suggestions. Orden must now be a hostage and his life must depend on the peacefulness of this community. His life must depend on the lighting of one single fuse on one single stick of dynamite."

He reached into his pocket again and brought out a little folding book, and he flipped it open and laid it in front of the colonel. "This, sir, was the answer to my report from headquarters. You will notice that it gives me certain authority."

Lanser looked at the little book and he spoke quietly. "You really did go over my head, didn't you?" He looked up at Corell with frank dislike in his eyes. "I heard you'd been injured. How did it happen?"

Corell said, "On the night when your lieutenant was murdered I was waylaid. The patrol saved me. Some of the townsmen escaped in my boat that night. Now, Colonel, must I express more strongly than I have that Mayor Orden must be held hostage?"

Lanser said, "He is here, he hasn't escaped. How can we hold him more hostage than we are?"

Suddenly in the distance there was a sound of an explosion, and both men looked around in the direction from which it came. Corell said, "There it is, Colonel, and you know perfectly well that if this experiment succeeds there will be dynamite in every invaded country."

Lanser repeated quietly, "What do you suggest?"

"Just what I have said. Orden must be held against rebellion."

"And if they rebel and we shoot Orden?"

"Then that little doctor is next; although he holds no position, he's next in authority in the town."

"But he holds no office."

"He has the confidence of the people."

"And when we shoot him, what then?"

"Then we have authority. Then rebellion will be broken. When we have killed the leaders, the rebellion will be broken."

Lanser asked quizzically, "Do you really think so?"

"It must be so."

Lanser shook his head slowly and then he called, "Sentry!" The door opened and a soldier appeared in the doorway. "Sergeant," said Lanser, "I have placed Mayor Orden under arrest, and I have placed Doctor Winter under arrest. You will see to it that Orden is guarded and you will bring Winter here immediately."

The sentry said, "Yes, sir."

Lanser looked up at Corell and he said, "You know, I hope you know what you're doing. I do hope you know what you're doing."

CHAPTER EIGHT

In the little town the news ran quickly. It was communicated by whispers in doorways, by quick, meaningful looks—"The Mayor's been arrested"—and through the town a little quiet jubilance ran, a fierce little jubilance, and people talked quietly together and went apart, and people going in to buy food leaned close to the clerks for a moment and a word passed between them.

The people went into the country, into the woods, searching for dynamite. And children playing in the snow found the dynamite, and by now even the children had their instructions. They opened the packages and ate the chocolate, and then they buried the dynamite in the snow and told their parents where it was.

Far out in the country a man picked up a tube and read the instructions and he said to himself, "I wonder if this works." He stood the tube up in the snow and lighted the fuse, and he ran back from it and counted, but his count was fast. It was sixty-eight before the dynamite exploded. He said, "It does work," and he went hurriedly about looking for more tubes.

Almost as though at a signal the people went into their houses and the doors were closed, the streets were quiet. At the mine the soldiers carefully searched every miner who went into the shaft, searched and re-searched, and the soldiers were nervous and rough and they spoke harshly to the miners. The miners looked coldly at them, and behind their eyes was a little fierce jubilance.

In the drawing-room of the palace of the Mayor the table had been cleaned up, and a soldier stood guard at Mayor Orden's bedroom door. Annie was on her knees in front of the coal grate, putting little pieces of coal on the fire. She looked up at the sentry standing in front of Mayor Orden's door and she said truc-ulently, "Well, what are you going to do to him?" The soldier did not answer.

The outside door opened and another soldier came in, holding Doctor Winter by the arm. He closed the door behind Doctor Winter and stood against the door inside the room. Doctor Winter said, "Hello, Annie, how's His Excellency?"

And Annie pointed at the bedroom and said, "He's in there."

"He isn't ill?" Doctor Winter said.

"No, he didn't seem to be," said Annie. "I'll see if I can tell him you're here." She went to the sentry and spoke imperiously. "Tell His Excellency that Doctor Winter is here, do you hear me?"

The sentry did not answer and did not move, but behind him the door opened and Mayor Orden stood in the doorway. He ignored the sentry and brushed past him and stepped into the room. For a moment the sentry considered taking him back, and then he returned to his place beside the door. Orden said, "Thank you, Annie. Don't go too far away, will you? I might need you."

Annie said, "No, sir, I won't. Is Madame all right?"

"She's doing her hair. Do you want to see her, Annie?"

"Yes, sir," said Annie, and she brushed past the sentry, too, and went into the bedroom and shut the door.

Orden said, "Is there something you want, Doctor?"

Winter grinned sardonically and pointed over his shoulder to his guard. "Well, I guess I'm under arrest. My friend here brought me."

Orden said, "I suppose it was bound to come. What will they do now, I wonder?" And the two men looked at each other for a long time and each one knew what the other one was thinking.

And then Orden continued as though he had been talking. "You know, I couldn't stop it if I wanted to."

"I know," said Winter, "but they don't know." And he went on with a thought he had been having. "A time-minded people," he said, "and the time is nearly up. They think that just because they have only one leader and one head, we are all like that. They know that ten heads lopped off will destroy them, but we are a free people; we have as many heads as we have people, and in a time of need leaders pop up among us like mushrooms."

Orden put his hand on Winter's shoulder and he

said, "Thank you. I knew it, but it's good to hear you say it. The little people won't go under, will they?" He searched Winter's face anxiously.

And the doctor reassured him, "Why, no, they won't. As a matter of fact, they will grow stronger with outside help."

The room was silent for a moment. The sentry shifted his position a little and his rifle clinked on a button.

Orden said, "I can talk to you, Doctor, and I probably won't be able to talk again. There are little shameful things in my mind." He coughed and glanced at the rigid soldier, but the soldier gave no sign of having heard. "I have been thinking of my own death. If they follow the usual course, they must kill me, and then they must kill you." And when Winter was silent, he said, "Mustn't they?"

"Yes, I guess so." Winter walked to one of the gilt chairs, and as he was about to sit down he noticed that its tapestry was torn, and he petted the seat with his fingers as though that would mend it. And he sat down gently because it was torn.

And Orden went on, "You know, I'm afraid, I have

been thinking of ways to escape, to get out of it. I have been thinking of running away. I have been thinking of pleading for my life, and it makes me ashamed."

And Winter, looking up, said, "But you haven't done it."

"No, I haven't."

"And you won't do it."

Orden hesitated. "No, I won't. But I have thought of it."

And Winter said, gently, "How do you know everyone doesn't think of it? How do you know I haven't thought of it?"

"I wonder why they arrested you, too," Orden said. "I guess they will have to kill you, too."

"I guess so," said Winter. He rolled his thumbs and watched them tumble over and over.

"You know so." Orden was silent for a moment and then he said, "You know, Doctor, I am a little man and this is a little town, but there must be a spark in little men that can burst into flame. I am afraid, I am terribly afraid, and I thought of all the things I might do to save my own life, and then that went away, and sometimes now I feel a kind of exultation, as though I were bigger and better than I am, and do you know what I have been thinking, Doctor?" He smiled, remembering. "Do you remember in school, in the *Apology?* Do you remember Socrates says, 'Someone will say, "And are you not ashamed, Socrates, of a course of life which is likely to bring you to an untimely end?" To him I may fairly answer, "There you are mistaken: a man who is good for anything ought not to calculate the chance of living or dying; he ought only to consider whether he is doing right or wrong."'" Orden paused, trying to remember.

Doctor Winter sat tensely forward now, and he went on with it, "'Acting the part of a good man or of a bad.' I don't think you have it quite right. You never were a good scholar. You were wrong in the denunciation, too."

Orden chuckled. "Do you remember that?"

"Yes," said Winter, eagerly, "I remember it well. You forgot a line or a word. It was graduation, and you were so excited you forgot to tuck in your shirt-tail and your shirt-tail was out. You wondered why they laughed."

Orden smiled to himself, and his hand went secretly behind him and patrolled for a loose shirt-tail. "I was Socrates," he said, "and I denounced the School Board. How I denounced them! I bellowed it, and I could see them grow red."

Winter said, "They were holding their breaths to keep from laughing. Your shirt-tail was out."

Mayor Orden laughed. "How long ago? Forty years."

"Forty-six."

The sentry by the bedroom door moved quietly over to the sentry by the outside door. They spoke softly out of the corners of their mouths like children whispering in school. "How long you been on duty?"

"All night. Can't hardly keep my eyes open."

"Me too. Hear from your wife on the boat yesterday?"

"Yes! She said say hello to you. Said she heard you was wounded. She don't write much."

"Tell her I'm all right."

"Sure—when I write."

The Mayor raised his head and looked at the ceiling and he muttered, "Um—um—um. I wonder if I can remember—how does it go?"

And Winter prompted him, " 'And now, O men——' "

And Orden said softly, " 'And now, O men who have condemned me——' "

Colonel Lanser came quietly into the room; the sentries stiffened. Hearing the words, the colonel stopped and listened.

Orden looked at the ceiling, lost in trying to remember the old words. " 'And now, O men who have condemned me,' " he said, " 'I would fain prophesy to you—for I am about to die—and—in the hour of death—men are gifted with prophetic power. And I—prophesy to you who are my murderers—that immediately after my—my death——' "

And Winter stood up, saying, "Departure."

Orden looked at him. "What?"

And Winter said, "The word is 'departure,' not 'death.' You made the same mistake before. You made that mistake forty-six years ago."

"No, it is death. It is death." Orden looked around

and saw Colonel Lanser watching him. He asked, "Isn't it 'death'?"

Colonel Lanser said, "'Departure.' It is 'immediately after my departure.'"

Doctor Winter insisted, "You see, that's two against one. 'Departure' is the word. It is the same mistake you made before."

Then Orden looked straight ahead and his eyes were in his memory, seeing nothing outward. And he went on, "'I prophesy to you who are my murderers that immediately after my—departure punishment far heavier than you have inflicted on me will surely await you.'"

Winter nodded encouragingly, and Colonel Lanser nodded, and they seemed to be trying to help him to remember. And Orden went on, "'Me you have killed because you wanted to escape the accuser, and not to give an account of your lives—!'"

Lieutenant Prackle entered excitedly, crying, "Colonel Lanser!"

Colonel Lanser said, "Shh—" and he held out his hand to restrain him.

And Orden went on softly, "'But that will not be as you suppose; far otherwise.'" His voice grew stronger. " 'For I say that there will be more accusers of you than there are now' "—he made a little gesture with his hand, a speech-making gesture—" 'accusers whom hitherto I have restrained; and as they are younger they will be more inconsiderate with you, and you will be more offended at them.' " He frowned, trying to remember.

And Lieutenant Prackle said, "Colonel Lanser, we have found some men with dynamite."

And Lanser said, "Hush."

Orden continued. " 'If you think that by killing men you can prevent someone from censuring your evil lives, you are mistaken.' " He frowned and thought and he looked at the ceiling, and he smiled embarrassedly and he said, "That's all I can remember. It is gone away from me."

And Doctor Winter said, "It's very good after forty-six years, and you weren't very good at it forty-six years ago."

Lieutenant Prackle broke in, "The men have dynamite, Colonel Lanser."

"Did you arrest them?"

"Yes, sir. Captain Loft and——"

Lanser said, "Tell Captain Loft to guard them." He recaptured himself and he advanced into the room and he said, "Orden, these things must stop."

And the Mayor smiled helplessly at him. "They cannot stop, sir."

Colonel Lanser said harshly, "I arrested you as a hostage for the good behavior of your people. Those are my orders."

"But that won't stop it," Orden said simply. "You don't understand. When I have become a hindrance to the people, they will do without me."

Lanser said, "Tell me truly what you think. If the people know you will be shot if they light another fuse, what will they do?"

The Mayor looked helplessly at Doctor Winter. And then the bedroom door opened and Madame came out, carrying the Mayor's chain of office in her hand. She said, "You forgot this."

Orden said, "What? Oh, yes," and he stooped his head and Madame slipped the chain of office over his head, and he said, "Thank you, dear."

Madame complained, "You always forget it. You forget it all the time."

The Mayor looked at the end of the chain he held in his hand—the gold medallion with the insignia of his office carved on it. Lanser pressed him. "What will they do?"

"I don't know," said the Mayor. "I think they will light the fuse."

"Suppose you ask them not to?"

Winter said, "Colonel, this morning I saw a little boy building a snow man, while three grown soldiers watched to see that he did not caricature your leader. He made a pretty good likeness, too, before they destroyed it."

Lanser ignored the doctor. "Suppose you ask them not to?" he repeated.

Orden seemed half asleep; his eyes were drooped, and he tried to think. He said, "I am not a very brave man, sir. I think they will light it, anyway." He struggled with his speech. "I hope they will, but if I ask them not to, they will be sorry."

Madame said, "What is this all about?"

"Be quiet a moment, dear," the Mayor said.

"But you think they will light it?" Lanser insisted.

The Mayor spoke proudly. "Yes, they will light it.

I have no choice of living or dying, you see, sir, but—
I do have a choice of how I do it. If I tell them not
to fight, they will be sorry, but they will fight. If I
tell them to fight, they will be glad, and I who am
not a very brave man will have made them a little
braver." He smiled apologetically. "You see, it is an
easy thing to do, since the end for me is the same."

Lanser said, "If you say yes, we can tell them you
said no. We can tell them you begged for your life."

And Winter broke in angrily, "They would know.
You do not keep secrets. One of your men got out of
hand one night and he said the flies had conquered the
flypaper, and now the whole nation knows his words.
They have made a song of it. The flies have conquered
the flypaper. You do not keep secrets, Colonel."

From the direction of the mine a whistle tooted
shrilly. And a quick gust of wind sifted dry snow
against the windows.

Orden fingered his gold medallion. He said quietly,
"You see, sir, nothing can change it. You will be
destroyed and driven out." His voice was very soft.
"The people don't like to be conquered, sir, and so
they will not be. Free men cannot start a war, but

once it is started, they can fight on in defeat. Herd men, followers of a leader, cannot do that, and so it is always the herd men who win battles and the free men who win wars. You will find that is so, sir."

Lanser was erect and stiff. "My orders are clear. Eleven o'clock was the deadline. I have taken hostages. If there is violence, the hostages will be executed."

And Doctor Winter said to the colonel, "Will you carry out the orders, knowing they will fail?"

Lanser's face was tight. "I will carry out my orders no matter what they are, but I do think, sir, a proclamation from you might save many lives."

Madame broke in plaintively, "I wish you would tell me what all this nonsense is."

"It is nonsense, dear."

"But they can't arrest the Mayor," she explained to him.

Orden smiled at her. "No," he said, "they can't arrest the Mayor. The Mayor is an idea conceived by free men. It will escape arrest."

From the distance there was a sound of an explosion. And the echo of it rolled to the hills and back again. The whistle at the coal mine tooted a shrill, sharp warning. Orden stood very tensely for a moment and then he smiled. A second explosion roared—nearer this time and heavier—and its echo rolled back from the mountains. Orden looked at his watch and then he took his watch and chain and put them in Doctor Winter's hand. "How did it go about the flies?" he asked.

"The flies have conquered the flypaper," Winter said.

Orden called, "Annie!" The bedroom door opened instantly and the Mayor said, "Were you listening?"

"Yes, sir." Annie was embarrassed.

And now an explosion roared near by and there was a sound of splintering wood and breaking glass, and the door behind the sentries puffed open. And Orden said, "Annie, I want you to stay with Madame as long as she needs you. Don't leave her alone." He put his arm around Madame and he kissed her on the forehead and then he moved slowly toward the door where Lieutenant Prackle stood. In the doorway he turned back to Doctor Winter. "Crito, I owe a cock to Asclepius," he said tenderly. "Will you remember to pay the debt?"

Winter closed his eyes for a moment before he answered, "The debt shall be paid."

Orden chuckled then. "I remembered that one. I didn't forget that one." He put his hand on Prackle's arm, and the lieutenant flinched away from him.

And Winter nodded slowly. "Yes, you remembered. The debt shall be paid."

For a complete list of books available from Penguin in the United States, write to Dept. DG, Penguin Books, 299 Murray Hill Parkway, East Rutherford, New Jersey 07073.

For a complete list of books available from Penguin in Canada, write to Penguin Books Canada Limited, 2801 John Street, Markham, Ontario L3R 1B4.